D1092495

SIGN OF EVIL

DI SARA RAMSEY 11

M A COMLEY

JEAMEL PUBLISHING LIMITED

New York Times and USA Today bestselling author M A Comley
Published by Jeamel Publishing limited
Copyright © 2021 M A Comley
Digital Edition, License Notes

All rights reserved. This book or any portion thereof may not be reproduced, stored in a retrieval system, transmitted in any form or by any means electronic or mechanical, including photocopying, or used in any manner whatsoever without the express written permission of the author, except for the use of brief quotations in a book review or scholarly journal.

This is a work of fiction. Names, characters, places and incidents are a product of the author's imagination or are used fictitiously, and any resemblance to actual persons living or dead, business establishments, events or locales is entirely coincidental.

 Created with Vellum

ACKNOWLEDGMENTS

Thank you as always to my rock, Jean, I'd be lost without
you in my life.

Special thanks as always go to @studioenp for their superb cover
design expertise.

My heartfelt thanks go to my wonderful editor Abby, my proofreaders
Joseph, Barbara and Jacqueline for spotting all the lingering nits.

Thank you also to my amazing ARC group who help to keep me sane
during this process.

To Mary, gone, but never forgotten. I hope you found the peace you
were searching for my dear friend.

ALSO BY M A COMLEY

Blind Justice (Novella)

Cruel Justice (Book #1)

Mortal Justice (Novella)

Impeding Justice (Book #2)

Final Justice (Book #3)

Foul Justice (Book #4)

Guaranteed Justice (Book #5)

Ultimate Justice (Book #6)

Virtual Justice (Book #7)

Hostile Justice (Book #8)

Tortured Justice (Book #9)

Rough Justice (Book #10)

Dubious Justice (Book #11)

Calculated Justice (Book #12)

Twisted Justice (Book #13)

Justice at Christmas (Short Story)

Justice at Christmas 2 (novella)

Justice at Christmas 3 (novella)

Prime Justice (Book #14)

Heroic Justice (Book #15)

Shameful Justice (Book #16)

Immoral Justice (Book #17)

Toxic Justice (Book #18)

Overdue Justice (Book #19)

Killer Blow (DI Sara Ramsey #2)

The Dead Can't Speak (DI Sara Ramsey #3)

Deluded (DI Sara Ramsey #4)

The Murder Pact (DI Sara Ramsey #5)

Twisted Revenge (DI Sara Ramsey #6)

The Lies She Told (DI Sara Ramsey #7)

For The Love Of… (DI Sara Ramsey #8)

Run For Your Life (DI Sara Ramsey #9)

Cold Mercy (DI Sara Ramsey #10)

Sign of Evil (DI Sara Ramsey #11)

I Know The Truth (A psychological thriller)

The Caller (co-written with Tara Lyons)

Evil In Disguise – a novel based on True events

Deadly Act (Hero series novella)

Torn Apart (Hero series #1)

End Result (Hero series #2)

In Plain Sight (Hero Series #3)

Double Jeopardy (Hero Series #4)

Criminal Actions (Hero Series #5)

Regrets Mean Nothing (Hero #6)

Sole Intention (Intention series #1)

Grave Intention (Intention series #2)

Devious Intention (Intention #3)

Merry Widow (A Lorne Simpkins short story)

It's A Dog's Life (A Lorne Simpkins short story)

Cozy Mystery Series

Murder at the Wedding

Murder at the Hotel

Murder by the Sea

A Time To Heal (A Sweet Romance)

A Time For Change (A Sweet Romance)

High Spirits

The Temptation series (Romantic Suspense/New Adult Novellas)

Past Temptation

Lost Temptation

Tempting Christa (A billionaire romantic suspense co-authored by Tracie Delaney #1)

Avenging Christa (A billionaire romantic suspense co-authored by Tracie Delaney #2)

PROLOGUE

*A*mber put the finishing touches to her makeup and admired the image she'd spent the last twenty minutes creating.

Is it over the top for the interview?

She admitted to being heavy-handed with the blusher, but one glance at her watch told her she really didn't have the time to fix it now.

She hitched on the snug jacket which matched her grey skirt and pulled up her tights after spotting a wrinkle in her left ankle. *I knew I should have bought the smaller size. Too late to worry about it now.*

Downstairs, she slipped into her high heels, and again, studied herself in the full-length mirror in the hallway. Then, she peered out of the window to see what the weather was like. It was January, the chances of it being warm were non-existent, but she knew wearing a coat would spoil the effect she was going for. *Decisions, decisions, but then, I'll be on a bus until the pick-up point, I should be okay, I hope!*

Nope, she was determined nothing was going to spoil her day. She needed this job, it would mean an end to all her debts within a few months. At nineteen, she pondered how she'd managed to get into so much debt in the first place. Ten grand, and for the life of her, she couldn't remember what she'd spent that money on. Except for a stylish collection of clothes and dozens of shoes filling her wardrobe.

Her friends were envious of her for her exquisite taste in fashion, but if only they knew the extent of her debt, she'd plummet in their estimation.

After another glance at her watch, she took deep breaths to calm the bout of nerves jarring her insides. "Here I go. Go get 'em, girl. I've got this. I'll have the interviewer eating out of my hands in no time at all," she chanted until her confidence trounced her anxiety.

Picking up her leather shoulder bag and the matching briefcase she'd recently splashed out on, she left the house with her shoulders back and walked to the end of the road to catch the bus into town. Her next stop would be to seek out a designated area near the precinct where a car would be waiting for her. The man she'd spoken to on the phone had told her the driver couldn't personally pick her up from the house because he was new to the area. She accepted the excuse, even felt guilty about it, Lord knows why.

She kicked herself for not having the courage to take driving lessons yet. All her friends drove, everyone except her. Maybe if she got the job, it would be a sign that she was growing in confidence—she hoped so.

As soon as she started working at Boots, her parents had informed her that she was on her own financially. As long as she put money in the housekeeping pot at the end of the month, she was welcome to live at home, but Amber was eager to break free. If she hadn't been as foolish with her money, maybe, just maybe, she would have been set up in her own flat by now. Still, she had her whole life ahead of her. She was aiming high with the job she'd set her heart on. The pay was fantastic and the temptation to travel to exotic countries with the owner of the business as his personal assistant proved to be too good an opportunity to turn down.

The bus showed up a few minutes after she arrived at the stop. She stamped her feet as she waited. The blast of cold air whipping around the corner made her shiver and cuss for not throwing her heavy coat on. *Damn idiot. Fashion over practicality will be the death of me one of these days.* She heaved out a relieved sigh when the bus came into view.

She smiled at the driver, handed him the correct change then tore through the bus to sit at the back. She rang her friend a few minutes later. "Hi, Sasha, I'm sitting on the bus. I'm so nervous, but also excited."

"Aww… you'll be great. You promised me you wouldn't get yourself worked up."

"I'm trying. What if I screw it up? Mess up all that stuff I have worked out in my head. What if it remains in there and refuses to come out?"

Her friend sniggered. "Don't be such an idiot. How many more times do I have to tell you to have confidence in yourself and your ability? If you have doubts, don't go."

Amber exhaled the breath she'd been holding in. "I can't not go. It's just a superb opportunity to do something good with my life. I'm young, but my philosophy is the younger you get on the right path, the more you're going to get out of life, right?"

"Of course. We've been over this a dozen times already. *Stop* stressing. Have you rehearsed what we said?"

"God, only like a trillion times. Here's hoping it comes out as intended. Shit! I must be insane going to this interview in the first place."

"Stop with the self-doubt, you hear me? You want me to come down there and give you a good slap? Because I will."

"Yeah, don't I know it? Okay, I'm gonna have to fly, my stop is coming up. Thanks again for all your support, Sasha, you're the bestest friend a girl could ever wish to have."

"Get outta here, you'd do the same for me. Good luck. Remember, stay calm and positive. They'd be absolute idiots not to offer you the job. Take care, stay safe."

I can always rely on Sasha to say the right thing, to throw cold water on my anxieties. "I love your confidence, wish I had an ounce of that instead of the fear that's running through my veins at the moment. Love you."

"Yep, love you, too. Ring me the moment you leave. I'll return your call as soon as the boss allows me to, okay?"

"That's a deal. Bye."

Amber ended the call and rang the bell, letting the driver know that she wanted to get off at the next stop. She waited until the bus came to a juddering halt rather than wobbling on her heels and looking like a fool. She headed through the swarm of shoppers in the precinct towards the prearranged pick-up point.

Her eyes almost dropped out of her head when she spotted the black limo standing there. She glanced around her. No, this couldn't be right. *I must be dreaming. This can't be for me!* She approached the car and the front door sprung open. A young man wearing a black suit and a chauffeur's cap jumped out of the car and half-bowed.

"Miss Rowse, I presume?"

"Umm, yes, that's right. Are you here to meet me?" It was a foolish question, given the fact he'd mentioned her by name. Her head was swimming.

He smiled and opened the rear door. "I'm Mick. Please, make yourself comfortable."

She climbed in the back, the soft leather beneath her resembling total luxury. He closed the door behind her and slipped into the driver's seat. "Help yourself to a drink."

Amber frowned and gasped as a flap dropped down in front of her to reveal an array of alcoholic and soft drinks. "That's very kind, I think I'm okay."

The door of the drinks cabinet rose again.

"Very well, Miss. Just relax and enjoy the ride."

She did just that.

The journey was the most comfortable ride she'd ever made, not surprising given her plush surroundings. Sadly, the trip was far too short. The driver pulled into an airfield and opened the door for her. She wriggled across the back seat and exited the car. "I don't understand, where am I?"

The chauffeur smiled and gestured towards the small plane adjacent to them, sitting on the tarmac. "Mr Barrows is awaiting your presence on board the plane. Enjoy your day."

"What? He said nothing about holding the interview on a *plane*. But…"

"I'm sure he'll explain all, once you're inside."

He got back in the car, leaving her with a dilemma. *What the heck! How can you hold an interview on a plane? What if he goes out of the country? I don't have my passport with me. Damn, did he mention in his emails that the interview would be held on a plane? I don't think so.*

Her stomach tied itself into knots. She hesitated for a moment longer until a young, handsome, slightly tanned and well-dressed man appeared at the top of the steps that led up into the plane. He gestured for her to join him. "Miss Rowse. It's an absolute pleasure to meet you. You're even more beautiful than in your photo."

His compliment distracted her long enough to ascend the steps. He shook her hand, and a jolt of excitement danced the length of her arm. "I… er… okay." Then, her stomach flipped again. She'd never flown before, not that she could remember. Her parents had taken her on holiday when she'd been two, but she had trouble recalling the experience.

If she was nervous about the interview before, it was nothing compared to what she was feeling now. Her legs trembled. Amber gripped the rail to help hold herself upright. Shaking legs and high heels were never a great combination.

He touched her elbow and guided her through the small cabin to a table with executive office chairs on either side.

"Come, take a seat. Can I get you a drink?"

"Would it be an imposition to ask for a coffee?" she asked meekly, minding her manners.

"Not at all. I have some brewing in the back. Milk or cream, and do you take sugar? I'm guessing not, not with a stunning figure like that to maintain."

Her cheeks warmed under his gaze. "One sugar and milk, please," she replied, doing her best to push his unexpected compliment aside.

No one had ever paid her this much attention, not even her regular boyfriend; she could get used to this. *What am I saying? This is purely business. But he's so handsome, it could lead to something else. Hush now, don't even go there.*

He returned, carrying two cups and saucers, and placed one in front of her. "Now, tell me all about yourself."

Personally or professionally?

"At present, I work in the make-up section at Boots."

"Yes, yes, I read as much on your application form." He took a sip from his cup, his piercing blue eyes never straying from her face. "If we're going to be working closely together, Amber, is it all right if I call you Amber?"

She nodded and took a sip of coffee.

"Okay, as I was saying, if we're going to be working closely together at all hours of the day, I need to know what drives you. What are your ambitions?"

"Oh my, I've never really thought what my aspirations entail, not long term. Short term, my aim is to better myself, you know, financially."

"Did you leave college with a mountain of debt?"

Her gaze dropped to her cup. "Not really. It's only since I started working, I fell into the trap. I've developed 'expensive tastes' my mum would say."

"Ah, that old chestnut, lavish existence on a poor man's pittance of a salary, right?"

She nodded. "Hence me trying my best to change my situation. I know I'm punching above my weight, applying for a job where I have very little experience, but I'm sure, if you give me a chance, I'll show you what my skills are worth before very long." She cringed at the way the words had tumbled out.

Judging by his amused expression, he'd possibly thought she'd thrown in a double entendre on purpose. His index finger tapped his thigh in a slow, deliberate beat. "I have no doubt about that. The moment I laid eyes on you, I could tell you're a woman with a vast amount of ambition. My question is, what are you willing to do to obtain such desires?"

Her chest tightened, and she frowned momentarily. "I don't under-stand. Sorry if I'm a bit dense." She winced. *Why the heck did I mention the word 'dense'?*

"We all have ambitions running through us, some more than others. All I'm asking is, what lengths are you willing to go to achieve your objectives?"

"I've never really thought about it. I suppose, given the opportuni-ties on offer, I would do what it takes to achieve them. If that makes sense?"

Another man entered the cabin, raised the steps and went through the door at the front of the plane. The next thing she knew, the engines had started up and they were taxiing down the runway. The panic washed over her and briefly took her breath away.

"What's going on? Why is the plane moving?" She peered through the window, and suddenly, the plane left the ground. She grappled for a seat belt, tugged and fastened it around her.

"Oops... my bad, maybe I should have pre-warned you. Not scared of flying, are you?"

"I... umm... I don't think so. Shouldn't you be wearing a seat belt?"

"Nah, I'm what's commonly known as a risk-taker. I trust my pilot implicitly. Often with my life."

"Good to hear. Sorry if you think I'm a wuss."

He cocked an eyebrow and smirked. "I don't. Drink your coffee."

She sipped at the now lukewarm drink and willed her nerves to settle. Her ears had popped several times already, which in itself, unnerved her. She hadn't prepared herself for this adventure, and she wasn't sure she was handling it the best way possible.

His head inclined. "You're confused, I can tell. What's rushing through your mind right now? Come on, total honesty."

"How scared I am. All I want is to sit here, and yet, I know you'll be expecting me to answer all your questions."

"All right, then. Why don't we skip the interview part and get down to the nitty-gritty of why you're really here?"

"Sorry?"

"What happens after work ends for the day?"

"I don't understand. I usually go home, is that what you meant?"

"There are fringe benefits to being on my payroll, Amber." A glint appeared in his mesmerising eyes. If only she knew what he meant by that statement.

"There are?" she asked, tentatively, resisting the temptation to gulp.

"Indeed. Here's the thing, I get lonely at night."

"Don't you have a girlfriend?" she asked, kicking herself for saying the dumbest thing that sprang into her mind.

"I have *lady* friends who visit me for evenings of pure delight, I wouldn't class them as girlfriends, though. So, I need to know that we're compatible... if you get my drift?"

What the fuck is he talking about?

"Meaning what, exactly?"

His smile slipped and was replaced by an evil sneer. "I'm proposing that you're going to need to spread your legs, regularly, if you want to work for me."

She swallowed down the acid scorching her throat. "No, sorry. That's impossible, I should have mentioned, I have a boyfriend. We're getting engaged soon, as soon as I've paid off my debts."

"So, what does that matter? I'm not bothered. Hey, considering the money that I'm offering for the position or *positions*..." He laughed at his suggestive joke. "Well, you should have realised there would be more to this role than just taking notes all day. Dump your boyfriend, come and be a part of my life. What do you say?"

Her saliva dried up and her voice shook when she said, "I'm sorry. This isn't how I expected the interview to go. I don't want to ditch my boyfriend, I love him. Where are we going? You haven't said." Her fear escalated, and turmoil erupted and coursed through her veins. *Why did I come here? Why?*

"Does it matter? Do you have another interview to go to today?"

"No, it's just that, umm... Greg is expecting me to meet him for lunch." It was a bare-faced lie, but the only thing she could think of saying that sounded plausible.

He sat back in his chair and folded his arms. "Okay, I suppose we should consider this interview terminated, then."

Even though she was irritated about how he thought she'd be okay with such an offer, she was willing to see past this, she didn't expect the opportunity to be taken away from her that easily. *I need this job, it could be the answer I'm searching for to become debt-free.* "What? Why? Because I have a boyfriend? That's not fair," she whined and then cursed herself for sounding childish.

He shrugged. "Life ain't fair, most of the time. You have a lot to learn if you think otherwise."

She shook her head in disbelief. *What now? What can I say to persuade him to turn the plane around?*

Placing a hand over her mouth, she retched. "Is there any chance we can turn back? I feel sick."

"No chance. You're here to stay."

Her stomach twisted several times. "What? What do you mean by that?"

He leaned in closer and gripped her knee. "You're *mine*. We're going to have fun. Just you and me."

"Please, I don't want this. I want to go home." Tears of frustration stung her eyes and she frantically glanced around her for an escape.

Sensing she was about to bolt, he grasped her wrist, tightly. "All in good time, once I've finished with you. Now, strip off, let's see what you have buried beneath that expensive suit of yours."

Sasha's words seeped into her mind and her confidence grew a touch. "I will *not*."

He leapt out of his seat, grabbed her knees and pried her legs apart. Then his hand shot up her skirt and ran the length of her thigh. Amber screamed, swiped his hand away, then sank into her chair and kicked out with her legs. He laughed at her failed attempts and then swooped, planting his wet lips over hers. She was taken aback; her eyes widened, fear freezing her in place.

He didn't care, his kiss deepened and his hands tore at her clothes. She struggled as much as her seat belt would allow.

He withdrew his mouth and positioned his nose against hers. "The more you struggle, the worse it's going to be." He caressed her throat and his hand slithered downwards until his finger traced the outline of her heaving breast. "Give in to it. I know you want me as much as I want you. I can tell by the look in your beautiful eyes."

"I don't. I swear this is all a terrible mistake. I'm happy with Greg. I'm sorry if you think there's been a misunderstanding. I only came here for an interview for a job."

He tipped his head back and let out a demonic laugh. "You fucking girls are all the same, prick teasers, the lot of you. Prancing around in tight short skirts, hitching them up when you sit down to reveal shapely thighs, and then, putting up the barriers once you've hooked us and reeled us in."

Flabbergasted, she opened her mouth to object, but the words failed to emerge. He lunged again, and this time his tongue invaded her mouth. She should have had the sense to bite down on it, instead, his kiss took her breath away, adding to her confusion.

He pulled back and rested his forehead against hers. "See, you're crying out for it, I can tell. Stop fooling yourself and give in to the desire."

"I don't. I want to go home. Please, please release me. I didn't sign up for this."

"You were seeking excitement and I've just offered it to you on a plate."

She shook her head and her eyes widened as her panic rose. "I don't want what you're offering me. I've told you, I'm happy with Greg."

"You're a *slut* who needs to be taught a lesson. What type of woman gets into a limo and climbs on board a plane with a stranger, eh?"

"I genuinely thought this was going to be an interview, and you had stopped off to see me between trips. It was an error on my part, please don't punish me."

"Keep begging, I like it." He glanced down at the bulge in his trousers, and Amber gulped. "Exciting, isn't it? Go on, admit you have a sexual attraction towards me."

"I don't. I love my—"

"*Boyfriend*. Yes, I've heard it all before. You're a *liar*. Now, remove the rest of your clothes."

"I refuse to."

Her attention was focused on his face; the hatred she saw in his expression rattled her bones. She failed to see his fist until it connected with her jaw. Her head whipped to the side, jarring her neck. She raised her knee, hoping to locate his crotch, but her attempt was futile. He struck her, over and over again. Until she lost consciousness.

1

$\mathcal{S}$ara Ramsey was in a good mood as she drove into work that morning. Why shouldn't she be? Even though it was January and the weather had turned cold, freezing some days lately, she was content with her life as it was. In the couple of months since she and Mark had tied the knot, she had woken up every morning with a certain zest for life. Something she'd never dreamt would have been possible before Mark had swooped into her life, unexpectedly.

She smiled, remembering that day clearly. The day he'd saved her pussy, so to speak. Misty had been poisoned a few years before. Sara had been beside herself, fearing that if Misty died, she would lose her one last connection with her late husband, Philip.

Pulling up at the traffic lights, Sara wiped away a stray tear that had dripped onto her cheek. "Silly woman," she scolded herself. "Even now, after all this time, you can't think of him without feeling emotional."

She switched on the CD player and slotted into first gear at the sound of Luther Vandross' dulcet tones, filling the interior of the car.

Another five minutes, and she drew into her allocated parking space at Hereford Police Station. Sara exited the car, breathed in a lungful of cool fresh air she knew would help her combat the day ahead and then entered the main door.

"Good morning, Jeff. And how are you on this fine, frosty morning?"

The desk sergeant looked up from his paperwork and raised an eyebrow at her. "Umm… can't say I've really thought about it, Ma'am. I suppose, if I had to say something off the top of my head, it would be that my extremities are colder than anticipated. I guess one should expect that in January."

"That's a shame. As long as those extremities don't get too cold that they end up dropping off, you should be okay."

Jeff shook his head, a grin creeping in place. "You seem in fine fettle this morning, Ma'am, any particular reason?"

"I am. Is it too much to ask the universe not to throw anything at me which is likely to change that, or would that be deemed as pushing my luck?"

"Sorry, I'm not an expert on talking to the universe, so I'll have to pass on that one."

"You should try it sometime. I sincerely believe in it. Anyway, I must press on, I can't stand around here all day, gossiping. Are the team all here?"

"Except for a notable absentee, yes."

Sara frowned. "And who would that be?"

"Carla. Let's just say I haven't seen her waft through yet, although I did have to leave the desk unmanned a little while back, you know, when nature came a calling."

She pulled a face. "Er… too much information there, buster, thanks. I'll check first and chase her up if she hasn't arrived yet."

"Have a good day."

"You too." Sara punched the number into the security keypad and entered the inner sanctum. She raced up the stairs and into the incident room. Jeff had been correct in his assertion, Carla was nowhere to be seen. She glanced up at the clock; her partner still had ten minutes to get here before their official shift started. "Morning all, anyone heard from Carla since yesterday?" She tried her hardest to keep her concern to a minimum.

The team all glanced at each other and then back at her, all of them either shaking their head or shrugging. "Never mind, I'm sure she'll show up soon. I'll grab a coffee, anyone want one?"

Marissa left her seat to help distribute the drinks. Task complete, Sara went into her office and closed the door, but not before issuing the instruction to send Carla in to see her once she arrived.

A weird sensation pulled her insides in all directions. *Don't be such an idiot, stop over-thinking things, she's fine.*

Engrossed in her daily chore, she failed to hear the knock on the door, if there had been one. It opened to reveal DCI Carol Price. "Got time for a brief chat?"

"Sorry, I was fascinated by the latest policies coming down from the Head Office. Come in."

Carol chuckled and closed the door behind her. "Like I believe that. I take it you've received the same letter I had, that's why I'm here."

Sara picked up the letter and waved it. "Same old shit: cutbacks. Remind me again why I do this job? Why any of us bust a gut to arrest the criminals in this area when Head Office are so damn keen on cutting back our hours? What's the bloody point?" She flung the letter in the bin and slouched in her chair.

"Stop it! You hear me? Stop feeling so dejected. In my expert experience, they're testing us, seeing how far they can go before we snap."

"Seriously? Jesus, don't they have anything better to do than to test our limits? I have to tell you, I'm at the end of my tether on this one." She raised a finger. "That team out there give it their all. They have to, otherwise they get a frigging rocket up the arse from me." She shook her head, then exhaled with frustration and defeat. "You think revealing that one of them might get the sack soon will be welcome news? You're wrong. I'll tell you this, I'm not going to be the one to sack someone just so this department comes within the guidelines of the latest sham of a budget."

"Now, Sara, calm down. You'll have to do it. That type of pressure comes with the territory, you knew that when you accepted the role."

Sara sprang forward in her chair again and placed her elbows on the desk. "It sucks! S-U-C-K-S, sucks."

Carol rolled her eyes. "I'm aware of how to spell the word, thank you. You need to get over this and quickly, Sara."

"Or what? What if I refuse to kick someone out? Force them to quit and possibly say goodbye to the pension they have worked damn hard to accrue over the years, what then?"

Carol sighed heavily. "Then, I will have no alternative but to relieve you of your post."

"What? Are you for real? That's what all this comes down to?"

"Look, it's hard, you don't have to tell me that. Either we make the decision or…"

"Don't tell me, or it could be our jobs on the line, right?"

"That about sums it up perfectly, yes."

"Wow, I never, ever, thought I'd see the day, not in my time on the force. How long have I got before I have to make this life-changing decision? And no, that's not me being melodramatic, it's a fact. If I have to sack someone it's going to destroy their lives, as they know it." She shook her head in disgust. "I feel physically sick at the thought."

"It is what it is, Sara, get used to it."

"I'll never get used to exploiting people only to ditch them once they've outlived their usefulness."

"Bloody hell, that's a bit over the top, even for you."

"It might be. It happens to be the truth, though." She sighed and closed her eyes for a second before asking, "How long?"

"By the end of January. You're going to need to look through each of their records and ditch anyone who doesn't come up to scratch."

"I don't have anyone on this team who fills that criteria. All my people regularly bust a gut. Why us? You're always so fond of singing our praises and yet you're not prepared to speak up for us?"

"I stand by what I've always said: this team is the best in the area. The problem is Head Office are keen on number-crunching. The only possible way we can meet the new budgets they've put in place is by cutting the members of staff."

"It's just wrong, if you ask my opinion, not that it seems to be worth much these days, apparently."

"That's unfair and you know it."

"Is it? The team go above and beyond on each and every case we deal with, and this is the result. Talk about shitting your thanks."

Carol raised an eyebrow. "Maybe we should revisit this conversation another time."

"What, when I've managed to calm down? Here's news for you, boss, I'm not likely to. This is a damn disgrace."

"That's as may be. Nevertheless, it's a directive we need to adhere to." DCI Price rose from her chair and opened the door. "We'll discuss it further soon."

Sara shrugged, knowing there was no way she was about to win the battle she was being forced to contend with.

The door closed firmly behind the chief, but it was opened again within a few minutes. Sara glanced up from her paperwork and frowned. "Carla? What in God's name happened to you?"

Her partner crept into the room and gingerly took a seat. Her face was discoloured in several places. Sara leapt out of her chair and sat on the desk in front of Carla. "Don't start on me. I'm here, aren't I?"

"Barely, you can't come to work in that state and not expect me to be worried about you. Come on, what gives?"

Carla sucked in a shuddering breath. "I was attacked."

"Whoa, no shit, Sherlock, I gathered that much for myself. Sorry, bloody hell, girl. You poor thing. Who did it?"

"I don't know. Someone jumped me outside my house last night." Carla burst into tears.

Sara reached out and placed a hand on her shoulder. "Let it out, you'll feel much better after a good cry, my mum swears by it. Cures all evils, she says." She snatched a tissue from the box on her desk and muttered, "I can't believe this. Do you think it was a one-off or intentional?"

Carla's gaze met hers. "I don't know. The attacker didn't say anything, never mentioned me by name, so I haven't got a clue."

"All right. We'll get whoever did this to you, love, don't worry."

"How do you propose doing that? I didn't see the person. They wore a balaclava."

"Did you go to the hospital? To get checked over?"

"No. I don't want to make a fuss."

"A *fuss*? Are you bloody kidding? You can barely sodding move. That's it, we're going over there right now."

"No, Sara, please. I just want to forget it ever happened."

Sara closed her eyes and asked the obvious question. "Were you sexually assaulted in the attack?"

Carla buried her face in her hands and sobbed. "I can't answer that. I was out cold for a while. One of my neighbours found me lying just outside my front door. I'd managed to crawl there, not sure how. Everything is so blurry."

"Jesus, why come to work today? I can't allow you to be here. You're neither use nor ornament, hon."

"I'm staying. Don't force me to go home. I won't go."

"What? You want to stay here? Why?"

"It's where I belong. I need to be around my friends."

"I can't drag you along as my partner should a case come into our hands today."

"So be it. I have other uses, boss. I can get stuck into the research around here, someone else can tag along with you."

"You drive a hard bargain. What about getting checked over by the duty doctor?" Before Carla could say anything, she continued, "Yes, that's the answer. I'll see if he's around. No arguments. It's either that or I drive you home and lock you inside your flat."

"You can be such a nightmare at times. I'm sorry to be a burden. I couldn't stay at home. I came to work because I was too petrified to be alone. What if someone is out there and their intention was to kill me?"

"Was anything stolen? Your purse, handbag or phone in the attack?"

"No. Nothing. That's what is baffling me."

"Let me get you a coffee, the cure for all desperate situations, then I'll try to track down the duty doctor."

"Thank you, you're too kind."

Sara placed a hand on Carla's cheek. "You'd do the same for me. I've got your back, partner."

She darted out of the room. All the other members of her team stared at her as she emerged. "She's fine. She's come to the right place to get the help she needs. I know you're all concerned, but she's keen not to have any fuss. So get back to work, peeps."

Reluctantly, her colleagues put their heads down and got back to their daily grind. Sara bought a coffee from the vending machine, picked up the nearest phone and rang the front desk. "Jeff, it's DI Ramsey. Is the duty doctor around? Or do you know if he's due in any time this morning?"

Jeff tutted and blew out a breath. "It's awful. Carla looked dreadful. I tried to offer some form of help, but she brushed me aside."

"It wasn't intentional. I'm sure she appreciated your concern. Is he around, Jeff?"

"Sorry. No, I don't think so. Want me to give him a call?"

"Would you? She's refusing to go to the hospital. Stubborn in adversity and all that."

"If I was sexist, which I'm not, I'd be saying that's typical of a female officer."

Sara sniggered. "You know us so well. She's definitely taken a battering, that's for sure."

"Will you be running an investigation into the attack, Ma'am?"

"It depends if Carla wants to take it further or not."

"Try to persuade her. Whoever did this to her shouldn't be allowed to get away with it, they should be banged up." His concern touched a nerve.

"I hear you. I've got to get back to her now. Let me know what the doctor says."

"I'm on the case now."

Sara replaced the phone in the docking station.

"We're worried about her, boss," DS Jill Smalling whispered.

"I know. You're not the only one. She's in a terrible state, we'll do all we can to make things easier for her. Let her be the one to ask for help, okay?"

"She's a proud woman. Too proud sometimes. We all need help occasionally, she needs to accept it from her friends. That's what we are, not just colleagues but good friends as well."

"She knows that. Just be there when she chooses to open up. I'll get back to her and my dreaded post now. Thanks for caring, Jill."

"We all care, boss, all I'm doing is acting as spokesperson for the team."

Sara smiled and returned to her office. She set the drink down in front of Carla. "How are you feeling now?"

"Better. I'm not saying I'm ready to run a marathon just yet, but definitely on the mend."

Sara retook her seat, and the phone rang. "DI Sara Ramsey."

"It's Jeff, Ma'am. I've managed to locate the doc, he'll be here within the hour. That's the best he could do."

"That's fine. I'm sure we can cope until then. Send him up when he arrives, Jeff. And thank you."

"My pleasure."

Sara ended the call and glanced up to see Carla staring at the wall over Sara's shoulder. "Are you sure you're okay? You seem dazed. I can't believe you drove here in that state."

"I did. I took it steady." Carla's gaze remained on the wall. With a shaky breath she faced Sara and broke down. "Oh God, what have I ever done to deserve this?"

"Get that thought out of your head, you've done nothing. You have to believe this was a mistake, Carla, not intentional." She patted Carla's hand and sighed. "Are you sure the attacker said nothing to you to suggest otherwise?"

"The problem is, I can't bloody remember. I was too busy trying to shield myself to listen to him if he did speak." She took a deep breath, frowning. "Hang on, let me think about that for a second." She fell silent and frowned. Eventually, she shook her head slowly. "No, I'm sure he didn't. Why me?"

"I don't know. Maybe this man had anger issues and decided to take it out on the first person he came across."

"That sucks. If that was the case, then I'm glad he chose me and not some frail old man or lady; they would never have survived such a brutal kicking."

"He used his foot as well? Jesus, no wonder you're battered and bruised. I still think you'd be better off at home."

Carla sniffled and wiped her nose on the tissue Sara flung at her. "I can't do it. What if he comes back... you know, to finish the job off?"

"That's presuming he pinpointed you for a reason, love. We have yet to determine that. What time did it happen last night?"

Carla shook her head slowly. "I'm unsure. I think I got home at around seven. My neighbour found me at about nine."

"Jesus." Tears pricked her eyes. "Why didn't you call me? I would have come out to you last night. Bloody hell, Carla. You're a mess, no wonder the bruising has had a chance to come out. Have you slept at all?"

"Off and on during the night, in between turning over and wincing through the pain."

"Are you sure you can't think of anyone with a grudge against you?"

Her gaze lowered and rose again a few seconds later. "Only Gary."

Sara returned to her seat and sank back in her chair. "What? No, he'd never do this."

"I'm glad you have that much faith in him."

"Wouldn't you have recognised his physique?"

"Not necessarily. What if he outsourced the attack? Got one of his mates to rough me up a bit on his behalf."

"Do you want me to go there and have a word with him? I will, you know I will."

"No, leave it. Let things lie for now. See what the doctor says and then I'll deal with the consequences."

"You're so brave."

A smile touched Carla's lips. "I don't think that's the word. I'm going to let you get on now, I've held you up enough for one day."

"Nonsense. I can catch up on this, your well-being is paramount, love."

"The last thing I want to be is a hindrance. Shame we haven't got a case on at the moment, one I could sink my teeth into to take my mind off things."

"There's plenty of paperwork to do, if you're that eager." Sara winked.

Carla rose from her chair and winced. She took her drink with her. "I'll find something. Thanks for listening, Sara."

"I'm always here for you, you know that. Take it easy, see how you go. If you find it too much, then I'll get one of the lads to take you home."

"No," Carla replied sharply.

Sara sighed. "You're going to have to go home at some point. Can you stay with a friend for a few days?"

"I'll ask around. Leave it with me."

Sara watched her leave the room and exhaled a large breath. *What the hell? How could someone be so callous as to beat Carla up like that? She's never struck me as being a bad person. Maybe we should start looking over the cases we've dealt with recently, see if anyone comes to mind with a possible grievance against Carla.*

She reached for her phone, dialled Will's direct number and asked him to step into the office for a few minutes.

He entered the room not long after. "Yes, boss?"

"Take a seat, Will. I need you to keep quiet about this for now, got that?"

"Is this to do with what happened to Carla?"

"Yes. She doesn't know who or why the attack occurred. I've been thinking that maybe it could be connected to a previous case we've solved."

"And you want me to do some digging, is that it?"

"Discreet digging. Can you do that?"

"I can try. What if Carla asks me what I'm up to?"

"Tell her you're doing some research for me. We have a few cases about to go to court soon, so it's not beyond the realms of possibility, is it?"

"Okay. Didn't she recognise the attacker?"

"No. Not at all. It happened last night. She was out cold for a while, and a neighbour found her and helped her inside the house."

"It's sickening. I know she's split up with 'Fireman Sam' recently, what about him?"

"The jury is still out on him. I didn't know him well, but it might be worth paying him a visit during his shift. If nothing else, it'll send a message that we're onto him. Did that make sense?"

He smiled. "Yeah, in a roundabout way. Want me to have a chat with Craig or Barry, see if either of them will go and see him?"

"Again, it would have to be done on the quiet. If Carla got wind of what we were up to, there'd be hell to pay."

He tapped the side of his nose. "Leave it with me. Was there anything else?"

"I don't think so. Let me know what you find out at the end of the day, all right?"

Will stood and left her to her paperwork. She pushed it aside for a few minutes and reflected on what Carla had told her about the attack. Prayed that something would come to light soon. Until then, they had nothing. Her frustration mounted, she ran a hand through her hair and then knuckled down to work through the post again.

An hour later, her phone rang. "DI Sara Ramsey."

"It's Jeff, Ma'am. Two things for you: the first is that the doctor has arrived, he's asked to see Carla down here, in one of the interview rooms. He thinks it'll be more private for her."

"I'll send her down in a mo. What's the second?"

"I've just had a call about a possible kidnapping and wondered if you'd be interested in the case."

"Why not? It's not as if we have anything else on at the moment. Tell you what I'll do, I'll escort Carla downstairs to see the doctor and drop by to see you, you can fill in the details, then."

"I like your thinking, killing two birds."

"I try my best, Jeff."

She ended the call and shot out of her chair. "Carla, we've got an appointment."

Carla glanced her way and her brow furrowed. "We have?"

"Correction, you have. The duty doctor wants to see you downstairs. I'll come with you."

Carla's eyes rolled up to the ceiling and she struggled to her feet. She teetered a little.

Craig, ever the gent, shot out of his chair to steady her.

She smiled at him. "Thanks. I'm fine, just a bit tender around the middle."

Sara and Carla exited the incident room and took a slow walk down the stairs. They parted at the bottom. "I'll come and see what the doc says in a second, after I've had a word with Jeff about the new case."

"I'll be fine, you don't have to mollycoddle me."

"I wasn't aware I was." She smiled and continued, "Perhaps I'm guilty of doing a little of that. It's only because I care."

"I know you do. I'd better not keep him waiting."

Carla turned and walked down the narrow corridor. Before she entered the room at the end of the hall, Sara watched Carla hesitate. After one final glance in her direction, her partner stepped into the room, and Sara went to have a word with Jeff.

"What have we got? I know we don't generally deal with kidnappings, saying that we had that case this year. Bugger, ignore me."

Jeff laughed. "It was because of the Laura Taylor case being prominent in my mind that I rang you."

"You did right." She leaned forward and whispered, "We're twiddling our thumbs up there, and no, those words never left my lips."

Jeff sniggered. "Your secret is safe with me. Here are the notes I jotted down. I received a call from Aiden Rowse who said his nineteen-year-old daughter, Amber, hasn't been seen since Monday morning."

"Okay, that's forty-eight hours ago. Why the delay in reporting her missing?"

"A bit of confusion between the parents, they work different shifts."

"I see, so they're like ships passing in the night and never get time to discuss family life, right?"

"So it would appear, Ma'am."

"Okay, we can sort that out later. Give me the address. I'd rather make my own assumptions about people once I've spoken to them."

He handed her a sheet of paper with their contact details. "I'll ring them in a second." She peered over her shoulder at the corridor.

"Has she said anything?" Jeff asked.

"Not really. She hasn't got a clue who attacked her. She's in a right state. I told her to go home, but she's too scared to."

"I'm not surprised. If she hasn't got anywhere else to stay, Wendy and I can put her up for a few days."

"That's kind of you, Jeff. I'll let her know." Sara smiled and made her way down the corridor where Carla was. She lightly tapped on the door and opened it. "Can I come in?"

The doctor shrugged and looked at Carla. "Your choice."

Carla nodded. "Of course, come in."

Sara closed the door behind her and pulled up a chair next to Carla. "What's the damage, Doc?"

"The damage actually appears to be minor, although the bruising makes things seem a thousand times worse."

Sara squeezed Carla's hand gently. "That's good news. No broken bones to contend with, you must be relieved, love."

Tears welled up in Carla's eyes. "I am, but it hurts like hell."

The doctor nodded. "I'll give you some painkillers to dull the pain. I've told her she shouldn't be here."

"I echoed that sentiment, she's adamant, though. I'll ensure she remains on desk duties for the next few days, if that will help?"

"It will, if she's too stubborn to stay at home."

"What about her ribs? Since she's struggling to move properly, my guess is they took a hammering."

"Yes, I've told her it would be better if she went to hospital to have an X-Ray, but she's refusing; there's very little I can do to change her mind. I take it you haven't had much luck in that department either, hence the reason you called me in to take a look."

"Exactly. I'll take good care of her, I promise."

He scribbled out a prescription and slid it across the desk to Carla.

"Take one tablet every four hours. If the pain persists, give me a call. That's an order, you hear me?"

Carla issued a taut smile. "I promise."

The doctor left the room. "Desk duties for you for the next few days, my girl. Do you want me to nip out and get your prescription for you?" The pharmacy was only a few doors away, no great hardship to Sara.

Carla eyed her sheepishly. "Would you mind? Oh no, what am I thinking? What about the new case?"

"I'll deal with that once I've got you settled, no arguments."

"As if I dare. I'm so damn emotional right now, on the verge of crying all the time. I'm grateful for your support, Sara."

"Get away with you! Want to stay here until I get back or can you make it upstairs by yourself?"

"If I take my time, I'm sure I'll be fine."

Sara opened the door and was tempted to help Carla to her feet, but she restrained herself from smothering her friend and colleague. Again, they parted at the bottom of the stairs.

Sara trotted down the road to the pharmacy and paid for the prescription. She returned and stood hovering over Carla until she downed her first tablet, then she announced, "Okay, we all know that Carla is indisposed at the moment, so who fancies stepping up to the plate and becoming my substitute partner for the next day or so?"

Both the youngsters, Marissa and Craig, thrust their hands in the air. "I'd love the opportunity, boss," Marissa announced.

"Me too," Craig added.

Sara studied them both, her mind going over their specific abilities. In the end, she plumped for Craig. "Sorry, Marissa, your input on the research side of things is too valuable around here."

Marissa's head dipped. "I understand. Maybe you'll bear me in mind in the future, boss?"

"That goes without saying. Craig, grab your coat. Carla's in charge in my absence, be gentle with her, she's had enough mauling for one day."

The team, including Carla, all laughed. "Ouch, did you have to say that?"

"Sorry. Okay, we'll be off now. As soon as we learn anything, I'll be in touch. All I know at present is that Amber Rowse went missing around forty-eight hours ago."

"Wow, why so long before contacting the police?" Carla asked, voicing the same question that had crossed her own mind.

"Parents on opposite shifts. That's all I know."

*I*n the car, Craig settled into his seat and fell quiet. "One rule if you partner me," Sara said.

"What's that, boss?"

"You don't sit there like a moron. We don't really know each other that well yet, but let's see if we can change that."

She heard him gulp noisily. "Umm… what is it you want to know?"

"What makes you tick? I know everything there is to know about your academic achievements, they're in your personnel file. I want to know about *you*."

He sucked in a breath and let it out slowly as he thought. "I suppose I don't really get much spare time, but when I do, I prefer to spend it with my girlfriend, Jenny."

"There, see, I didn't even know you had a girlfriend. Look at the great strides we've made already. How long have you been together?"

"Blimey! I think it's about four years, give or take a few months. She's a fitness instructor, teaches yoga and holds regular classes down at the gym."

"In other words, she's fit," Sara chortled.

"In more ways than one. I'm hoping to pop the question soon. Can't imagine my life without her."

"How wonderful. Gosh, I'm filling up here, I needed to hear some good news after what we've been confronted with this morning."

"You're not wrong. It's scandalous what happened to Carla. If someone chose to attack one of us, is there any hope to keep the rest of the people in Hereford safe?"

"My thoughts exactly. My take is that she was specifically targeted; all we need to do now is find out who, and we'll be laughing."

"Was she examined for possible DNA?"

Sara shot a glance his way and then turned to combat the traffic ahead of her. "Shit! I never even thought about that. I bet she didn't either."

He fished his mobile out of his pocket. "Want me to ring her?"

"No. I'll deal with it when we get back. Although, I'm guessing what her answer is going to be. 'Don't make a fuss, I'm fine'."

"I bet you're right on that one. I suppose we'd be saying the same thing, if we were in her shoes, right?"

"Probably. Okay, let's leave that for now and focus on the task in hand."

She drew up outside a quaint cottage on the outskirts of town at Sutton St Nicholas. It had a pretty front garden, one side partially laid to lawn and the other decorated in slate chippings with small clumps of grasses dotted around, adding a certain amount of interest to an ordinarily dull January garden.

Sara rang the bell and got ready to show her ID. A man in his fifties opened the door. His stomach was rounded and strained his T-shirt. "Mr Rowse? I'm DI Sara Ramsey and this is my partner, DC Craig Watson."

"I'm so relieved you're taking my claim seriously. Please, come in. My wife is in the kitchen. Do you want a drink?"

"Thanks. Two coffees would be wonderful. How are you both holding up?"

"I'm not sure we are. Kathy keeps bursting into tears every time I speak. It's hard knowing what to say for the best, it's as though she wants to deny all knowledge of Amber going missing. The fact is, she's gone and we don't have a clue where."

"Okay, try and remain positive, we're going to do our very best to find her."

"I hope so. I don't even want to consider what the consequences might be. I run a pub, I see the way some men look at girls these days. I know that's a generalisation, but if you match that to the statistics of rapes or indecent assaults going on in this shitty world of ours, is it any wonder I'm going out of my mind with bloody worry about her?" He paused at the end of the hallway and added quietly, "Of course, I wouldn't mention any of that in my wife's presence."

"I understand. Please, you mustn't let your mind wander. Stick with what you know, I'm sure you'll both be reunited with Amber soon."

"Can I quote you on that?" He offered a faint smile and opened the door to the kitchen. A woman with shocking red hair that had obviously come out of a bottle, was standing at the stove, stirring a pot. She wiped her hands on her apron and came towards them. "Hello, I'm Kathy. Please, please tell me you're not going to give up on us."

"Of course we won't. I'm DI Sara Ramsey and this is my partner, DC Craig Watson. Can we take a seat?"

"You sit down, love," Mr Rowse instructed his wife. "I'll make the nice officers a drink. Do you want a coffee?"

"No, I've had my share for the morning already."

Kathy motioned for Sara and Craig to sit at the round kitchen table.

"Perhaps we can start with when you noticed your daughter was missing?" Sara asked.

Kathy placed her hands over her face. "Aiden works really long hours at the pub, he's got the day off today. I work four nights a week as a nurse at the hospital. This is the first opportunity we've had to spend time together all week. I asked in passing if he'd seen Amber, and he told me he hadn't spoken to her since Monday."

"And that's unusual, is it? To not see her?" Sara asked.

"Yes, she's always here. Well, most days, when she's not staying over at Greg's, that's her boyfriend."

"I take it you've contacted Greg?"

"Yes, he told us he hasn't seen her either, and he's tried calling her several times but her phone always goes into voicemail."

Sara saw Craig jot the information down out of the corner of her eye. She was grateful that she hadn't needed to ask him to do it.

"What about her friends, have you tried calling them?"

Kathy and Aiden glanced in each other's direction, their expression one of helplessness. "We've tried to think of her friends' names, but all her contact details are in her phone."

"Maybe she has a notebook or similar in her room?"

"I checked, I couldn't find anything," Kathy replied, downhearted.

"Okay, don't worry about it. Maybe Greg will be able to fill in some blanks there. Do you have his phone number?"

"We have his address, if that will do?" Aiden nudged his wife, expecting her to supply it.

"Yes, his Mum works with me. I'll get it for you, he still lives with Sandra."

"Okay. What about social media, have you checked her profiles? Has she been active on them since Monday?"

"I checked her Facebook and Instagram accounts and no, there've been no posts from her," Kathy confirmed from the other side of the room. She rummaged around in a drawer, withdrew a notebook and returned to the table. She flipped it open to the letter B and slid the book across the table to Craig. "Greg and Sandra Bishop, that's their home number. I'm sorry, I don't have their mobile numbers'. I really wish I did now."

"It's okay, we can sort that out, don't worry. What about work? Or is Amber at university?"

"No, she works at Boots on the Estee Lauder make-up counter."

"Have you checked to see if she's shown up there for her shifts? Is she full-time?"

"She enjoys her job but is always on the lookout for something better. I rang Boots and they hadn't seen her since Saturday. That was her final shift for them. They said she took a day's holiday on Monday."

Sara frowned. "I see, and you weren't aware of that?"

"No. She didn't tell us. Which makes matters worse. All I keep thinking is that she didn't trust us enough to tell us where she was going and now..." Kathy broke down and Aiden slung an arm around her shoulder to comfort her.

"Please, try and not get upset. We hear so many instances where teenagers take off without their parents' knowledge."

"Yeah, and how do those cases usually turn out?" Aiden was quick to fire back.

"More often than not, the teenagers were just out to prove a point to their parents."

"There was no need to do that, not with us," Kathy sniffled. "She's a good girl. She's not one of these girls who strut around in a huff if they don't get their own way. We treat her like an adult, she contributes to the household expenses. She's always cautious with her money, at least, I think she is."

Sara sensed some doubt filtering into Kathy's words. "Is there something that has come to mind, Kathy?"

Aiden grunted. "I think what my wife is getting at is that Amber has a penchant for nice things, you know, shoes, bags and designer clothes."

"Ah, so there could be a money issue, is that it?"

Kathy's chest inflated with a deep breath. "Yes, Aiden is right. She's never let us down with her rent, but I think sometimes, around the end of the month, she struggles to make ends meet. Isn't that normal with teens, though?"

"Possibly. Do you know who she banks with? It might be worthwhile taking a peek at her bank statements, see what state her finances are truly in."

"You think her expensive tastes could have led to debts that she kept hidden from us?" Aiden asked.

"There's a possibility of that, although it's purely speculation on my part until we gain access to her accounts."

"She's with the Halifax," Kathy replied.

Aiden ran a hand through his hair. "If she was in debt, she should have come to us. Maybe we're guilty of pushing her too hard too soon. Oh God, why didn't she come to us, talk to us?"

"Please, until we've seen what state her finances are in, there's no point blaming yourselves," Sara did her best to allay his fears.

"The inspector is right, love. Please don't do that, we're suffering enough as it is already."

"Do you want me to search her room, try to find a bank statement for you?" Aiden offered, already jumping out of his seat.

"It would make our lives easier if you could find something for us."

He set off and thundered up the stairs and into the room above the kitchen. Sliding wardrobe doors banged.

Kathy rolled her eyes. "He won't find anything, he's a typical bloke, rarely sees what's under his nose. I'd better go and help him."

Sara smiled and nodded. Kathy left the room.

"You think the girl has fallen into some kind of trap?" Craig asked.

"I'm not sure. The money aspect is definitely an eye-opener. I can't afford expensive clothes, handbags and shoes on an inspector's salary, so how is a mere shop assistant doing it?"

"Yeah, I suppose it depends on how much she pays her parents a week or month to live here. You have a mortgage and all the household bills to meet and cover every month."

"True enough. Although my mortgage is quite small in comparison to most, it's still a hefty wedge off my monthly income."

"What next? If they don't find anything?"

"We'll get on to the bank, and after that, we'll pay the boyfriend a visit. I wish we had a girlfriend's contact details, they usually hold the key in cases like this."

Craig lowered his voice and asked, "You think she's guilty of having secrets, the type you're keen to hide from your parents, right?"

"It's looking that way to me. Let's face it, at present, that's all we have to go on."

Craig flipped back through his notes. "Sadly, I think your assessment is correct, judging by what we've learned so far." He shuddered.

"What was that for?"

Again, keeping his voice low, he replied, "The thought of someone abducting her and doing unmentionable things to this teenager, it makes my skin crawl."

"That's because you're a sensitive man."

"I am? Maybe you should have a word with Jenny about that." He smiled.

They fell quiet when they heard Kathy and Aiden coming back down the stairs.

"Anything?" Sara asked, more out of hope than expectation.

"I found this under her bed." Kathy handed Sara a screwed-up bank statement which she flattened out on the table.

Sara read the contents and shook her head. "And you had no idea she was in this much debt?"

"No, she never told us. How can the bank allow her to be ten thousand in debt? I don't understand. Looking at the rates she's paying, that in itself is nothing short of being bloody criminal, it shouldn't be allowed."

"Ouch, I missed that part," Sara replied, scanning the statement again. "You're right, it's irresponsible for the bank to allow youngsters to notch up debts this large. As long as they get their cut, I suppose, everything is rosy to them."

"Shame on them. She has more debt than both of us put together. We've had to be super cautious with money over the years, neither of us chose a job that was ever likely to make us rich."

"It's hard to fathom what goes on in the heads of youngsters. I don't think they understand the term 'saving up for what you need'." Sara chuckled. "I know that makes me sound like my mother, but I think she has a point."

Kathy nodded her agreement. "Too right. We're the same, we don't have a loan to our name; if we can't afford it, we don't buy it, it's as simple as that. I'm guilty of letting my daughter down, she shouldn't have got herself into such a rut with money and now... it could have got her into a world of trouble, couldn't it?"

"No, love, I won't allow you to think that way. We can't run her life for her. We've always had an open relationship with her. I'm hurt that she's laden herself with these kinds of debts at such a young age. How many more kids are there out there in the same boat?" Aiden interjected, shaking his head.

"I should imagine a lot, Mr Rowse." Sara could sit there for hours, going over what she thought was right and wrong about the state of the economy and the effect it had on folks' personal finances, but it wasn't going to bring Amber back. She needed to crack on with the investigation. "What about a laptop, did she have one?"

"Yes, we bought her a second-hand one for Christmas last year. She uses it all the time. I think it's in the lounge. I'll be right back." Kathy raced out of the room and returned with a small black Lenovo laptop. She flipped the lid open and booted up the computer. Sara craned her neck to look at the screen. "Damn, I don't know her password, do you, Aiden?"

"How should I know? I wouldn't even know where to begin with a guess either."

Kathy tutted. "You're no bloody help. What about her boyfriend's name?" She tapped in *Greg*, but the password field juddered. "Shit!" She pushed the laptop away from her. "I don't know." Tears trickled onto her cheeks.

"It's okay. Please, you've done your best. If you'll allow me to take it, I'm sure Forensics will be able to get into it within a few minutes."

"Yes, take it. Of course, leave it to the experts, they're sure to know how to open it."

"Before we leave, is there anything else you can tell us? Maybe your daughter has mentioned someone showing an interest in her at work lately, something along those lines?"

"No, not that I can think of," Kathy admitted. She dried her eyes on a tissue and blew her nose.

"If she'd told me that I would have throttled the person," Aiden added.

"What type of character is she?" Sara asked.

"Gosh, loving, caring, and one that gets into a heap of debt without us knowing," Kathy added dejectedly.

"Don't go there, love. Once she's home, we'll sit her down and get all this sorted. It's not the end of the world."

Kathy gasped. "What if she owes money to someone unscrupulous and they've kidnapped her, intending her to work for them, you know, until the debt is paid off?"

"Please, it would be better for you not to think along those lines. I'm sure there's a simple explanation why she's gone missing."

"Really? But she had no reason to just disappear, simple explanation or not, it galls me to think she's been missing for two days and we didn't even realise. What does that say about us as parents?" Kathy broke down again.

Aiden comforted his wife once more. "Busy people, love, trying to earn money to keep a roof over our heads. We weren't to know that she would need us..."

"We'll find her. I'm sure all this will turn out to be a misunderstanding in the end."

"I hope so," a tearful Kathy replied. She buried her head into her husband's chest.

He ran a hand over her hair and made a soothing noise, peppered with the odd kiss on her forehead.

"I'm going to leave you a card, if you think of anything I should know, don't hesitate to ring me." Sara and Craig rose from their chairs.

Kathy remained seated and glanced up at Sara. "Please, do your best to find her."

"You have my assurance on that. We'll see what the laptop reveals, hopefully it'll give us a trail to follow which will bring your daughter home where she belongs."

Aiden led the way out of the kitchen to the front door. He shook their hands and added his own plea, "Do your best for our baby, promise me?"

"I promise you. My team is top-notch, we give our all to every case that comes our way. Take care of your wife, sir. If you have any joy remembering her friends' names, please let me know."

"Of course. Thank you, both of you. All we want is our daughter home safe and well. We don't care what sort of problems she's having to deal with, we can resolve those once she's home with us."

"That's good to hear, keep thinking positively and never lose your faith in us, that's all I ask."

"You've got it."

Aiden closed the door gently behind him. "Right, back to the car. I'm torn now, whether we should take the laptop to the lab first or go to see the boyfriend."

"If I was in charge, I think I'd be doing all I could to search for clues." He tapped the laptop lid.

"Decision made, then. The lab isn't too far, about twenty minutes or so. Why don't you ring ahead, let them know we're on our way and the urgency behind our visit?"

Craig carried out her instructions while Sara drove to the lab. When they arrived, there was a male technician waiting at the reception area for them.

"It's urgent we get a look at the young lady's movements ASAP. She's already been missing two days."

"Leave it with me. I should have this baby cracked open within the hour. Do you have a card? I'll contact you the minute I gain access."

"Thanks, that would be great. In the meantime, we'll get back on the road. We have friends and family to question."

"I hope it goes well for you. I'll be in touch soon." The technician, in his forties, smiled and turned to leave. He slipped through the security door and waved once he was on the other side.

Back in the car, Sara punched Greg's address into the satnav and set off. They pulled up outside a mid-terraced house that seemed tatty on the outside. The garden was a sharp contrast to the Rowses' and was littered with all kinds of debris, some of which, Sara surmised, would be hard to decipher without a forensic examination.

A young man in his late teens to early twenties answered the door. His hair was messed up and looked as though they had just woken him up.

Sara presented her ID, and he peered at it through half-closed eyes. "DI Sara Ramsey and this is DC Craig Watson. I take it you're Greg Bishop. Would it be possible for us to step inside for a little while?"

"Not until you tell me what this is all about. I've done nothing wrong to warrant the police knocking on my door."

"We're not saying you have. It would be better if we spoke inside."

His cheeks puffed out, and he stepped back. "Excuse the mess. My parents are away on holiday. I don't need to tidy up until Friday, they're due back on Saturday."

"I see. Had a few parties in their absence, have you?"

"You could say that. What's this about?"

"You want to discuss this in the hallway?"

"Come through to the lounge, you'll regret it, though."

He wasn't wrong. There was a quilt turned back on the sofa, and empty plates, dozens of glasses and cans were on every conceivable surface. "Good luck cleaning this up before your parents come back. I predict you'll need an army of cleaners to combat this mess."

"Thanks, not what I wanted to hear. Maybe I've been a fool, we had fun though, so totally worth it. Want me to clear a couple of chairs for you?"

"No, I think we'll be better off standing, thanks. We're making enquiries about your girlfriend, Amber."

He smirked. "I know her name, I've only got the one. And before you say it, yes, I know she's missing, and yes, I have been out there searching for her."

Sara doubted the truthfulness behind his claim. "I'm presuming you haven't had any luck on that front?"

His nose wrinkled and his lip curled up. "Would you be involved if I had?"

"Point taken. What we need to know is if you can think of anywhere Amber is likely to be right now."

"Haven't got an effing clue. She could have run off with another bloke for all I know."

Sara frowned. "Is that likely? Were the two of you having problems?"

"No, not that I know of. She's a cool bird, umm... girl. We're close, but not that close."

"Meaning what?"

"Meaning, I'm not her keeper. I don't keep tabs on her daily. She's free to do what she wants, when she wants. Clear enough for you?"

"Cut the attitude," Craig warned.

Greg shrugged his slim shoulders. "Sorry, but I get a sense where this is going. I know how these things work. You're going to come down on me for not caring about my girlfriend, which ain't true. I care enough, but I'm not her keeper."

Sara didn't like this boy, not at all. She sensed he was hiding something. "Yeah, that's twice you've told us that, we heard you the first time. What's going on, Greg?"

"What are you talking about? Nothing. What? You think I have something to do with her disappearance? That's *insane*. She's free to live her life how she wants to live it."

"Again, what is that supposed to mean? What are you trying to say?"

"I'm not *trying* to say anything, I've been honest and open with you. We go out with each other, but she's still free to see other people, that includes *other* men."

"Are you saying that she has other relationships?"

"No, you're twisting my words. Oh God!" He ran a hand through his hair, messing it up even more. "I can't stop her, or any girl, from having other male friends, and I wouldn't want to. I'm not the possessive type, is that any clearer?"

"Yes, thank you for clarifying the issue. In that case, may I ask when you last saw or spoke to her?" Sara held his gaze for a moment, trying to figure him out.

"Sunday, we went to the pub in the evening."

"And what sort of mood was she in?"

"Same as usual, no, wait, she did seem a little quiet, as though she had something on her mind. I didn't probe, and no, it's not because I don't care. People are entitled to have their quiet times, I appreciate that."

"I get that," Sara admitted. "Did this distraction manifest itself over your last few dates or did it appear just on Sunday?"

He paused to consider his answer for a moment. "No, just on Sunday, not that we see each other much, not lately."

"How often?" she probed, trying to get a better indication of their relationship.

"Once or twice a week. We both lead busy lives, you know, what with one thing and another. I have my mates, she has hers, we go on dates in between spending time with our pals."

"Have you been together long?"

"Around six months."

Sara nodded, she couldn't make her mind up about Greg. His concern appeared to waiver. "Her friends, can you give me their contact details?"

"You think I'd have them? Amber would be suspicious of me if I had her friends' numbers in my phone."

"Ah, okay. I never thought of it that way. Can you at least tell me some of their names?"

"Do you think they'll know where she is?"

"Possibly. We're going to need to speak to them first, to find out what they know, if anything." She withdrew her notebook and pen from her jacket pocket.

"Her best pal is Sasha."

Sara jotted down the name and then looked up at him. "Does Sasha have a surname?"

"Now you're testing me. It begins with M, let me think about it. I think it has to do with a fish..." His eyes screwed up as he searched his mind for the information and then he smiled and nodded. "I've got it. I think it's Minnow."

Sara scribbled the name down and glanced up at him. "I don't suppose you know where she lives?"

"Towards town, maybe around the park, the one near the college. Amber has mentioned that they used to walk around there sometimes when they were bored rather than stay at home."

"Aylestone Hill area, then?" Sara's impatience was starting to show in her words.

"Yep. I believe so." Greg watched Craig circulate the room, his eyes narrowing a little.

Sara drew his attention back to her. "Thanks for that, it'll make life a bit easier for us. What about her other friends, any luck with remembering their names?"

"Not really, Sasha is her best friend, the one she spends most time with. I wouldn't have a clue about any of the others."

"That'll do for now, then. What about any problems Amber might have had recently, did she confide in you at all?"

"Sort of. I can't recall anything, not really. She stressed about the hours Boots expected her to work now and again, you know, filling in for people if they were on holiday on top of her normal shifts. But then, she got on with it and said she needed the money."

"But basically, she was happy in her job, her career?"

"Yeah, as far as I know, apart from what I just said."

"Are you aware of her having any money troubles?"

His head inclined. "Should I be? Does she?"

"I take it that's a no, then?"

"It's a no. How much are we talking here?"

"It's not my place to say. If she'd wanted you to know, she would've told you. I'm not about to break any confidences."

"Oh right, pardon me for bloody asking, then. Jeez!"

"Sorry, I didn't mean to offend. I'm sure you understand the predicament I'm in. I have to ask questions without breaking any confidences."

"Yeah, I suppose I can understand that. Do you need anything else?"

"No, I think we're done here. All right if I leave you my card? If you think of anything else I should know, you can ring me day or night."

"I'll do that. I hope you find her soon. Should I be worried about her? I mean, I'm worried, but how concerned should I really be?"

"I don't think it'll do anyone any good worrying about her. Maybe she found things a little tough right now and just took off."

"She's not the type, that's what's bugging me. Are you going to do one of those conferences on TV?"

"Yes, I'll see how the investigation progresses today. If nothing is forthcoming, then I'll consider making an urgent appeal to the people of Hereford tomorrow."

"Good. The thought of her being out there alone is getting to me big time. She'd never cope on her own, she's not the type. That's why I find it hard to believe she's missing. She loves her home comforts."

Sara sensed his concern, finally. "Are you saying you believe someone has taken her?"

He frowned and scratched his head. "Isn't that what you think?"

"Unless we have proof of that, then it would be wrong of me to speculate anything other than her being a missing person. We really do need to know more about what has gone on in Amber's life in the past week or month."

"I wish I could tell you more, I can't. I feel such an idiot about that."

"It's okay. Maybe her friend Sasha can fill in the blanks for us. Thanks for speaking with us today."

"You're welcome. Please, find her."

His desperate plea surprised Sara. Maybe she'd misjudged his lack of concern throughout their conversation.

He showed them to the front door, and Sara rubbed his arm. "We'll do our very best."

Sara and Craig walked back to the car. Once inside she took out her phone. "I need to get an address for her friend. Something really stinks about this."

"Yeah, I thought it strange that the boyfriend couldn't really tell us much."

"According to what he said, I wouldn't really class theirs as a close relationship, would you?"

"No, I got that impression too."

"Jill, it's me. Can you do me a favour? Look up a Sasha Minnow, or a family of Minnows, living near the Aylestone Hill area." Sara fought hard to hold back the giggle tickling her throat.

Jill, ever the professional, thought nothing of it at her end and supplied her with an address within seconds. "Here you go, twenty-eight Baddington Road."

"You're a star. Once we've paid this young lady a visit, we'll return to base. Don't make it obvious I'm speaking about her, but how's Carla?"

"Fair to middling here, boss. We're all plodding on."

"Within earshot I take it?"

"That's right."

"Enough said, we'll see you soon."

hen they called at the Minnows' house, Mrs Minnow told them her daughter was at work, at a clothes shop situated in the centre of town. Sara had tried to reassure the woman that her daughter wasn't in any trouble, and they were conducting enquiries into an ongoing investigation, keeping Amber's name out of the conversation. This appeared to put the woman's mind at ease.

Sara and Craig entered New Look and approached the till area. "Hi, is it possible to speak with Sasha Minnow?" Sara asked the friendly woman behind the counter.

"Is this personal? We're not allowed to have personal visits during work hours, you see."

Sara produced her warrant card. "It's important. I'm DI Sara Ramsey. I appreciate this might be an inconvenience for you, but I can't leave it until she finishes work."

"Oh my, is she in some kind of trouble?"

"No, not at all. I need to ask her to help us with our enquiries, that's all. Is she here?"

"She's counting stock out the back. I'll take you through, if you like?"

"Thanks. It might be better to have a conversation out there."

The woman showed them through a narrow passageway to a large stockroom at the rear. They'd obviously had a recent delivery because there were piles of boxes everywhere. "Sasha, can you come here a minute, please?" the shop assistant called out.

Within seconds, a tiny girl with black hair appeared. "Yes, Joanne. I was in the middle of putting away the first delivery. Did you want me to do something else?"

"No. There are two police officers to see you. You can either see them here or go to the staffroom, there shouldn't be anyone in there at the moment."

Sasha's eyes darted between Sara and Craig. "I see. Maybe the staffroom would be better."

"Off you pop, then. Please, try not to take up too much of her time; as you can see, we're snowed under, and all this stock needs to be checked off by the end of the day. No mean feat, as you can imagine."

Sara smiled. "We promise to be as quick as possible."

The shop assistant, who Sara now assumed to be the manager or supervisor, left them to it.

"Come this way," Sasha requested.

The canteen was a cold, unwelcoming room that was in need of a good clean and lick of fresh paint.

"Take a seat. What's this about?" Sasha asked, flopping into a chair opposite Sara and Craig.

"Thanks for agreeing to see us. We're conducting enquiries into an investigation of a missing person, Amber Rowse."

Sasha's gaze immediately dropped to the table. "Oh, I see."

"When was the last time you spoke to her?" Sara leaned forward in an attempt to get Sasha to look at her.

"Umm... Sunday, I believe it was. Yes, around six."

"Not since then?" Sara watched Sasha wring her hands.

"No, not at all. Missing you say?" the young woman replied, her tone flat.

"That's right. We're trying to ascertain if she had any problems or if something was likely concerning her. Did she?"

Without looking up, Sasha shrugged and shook her head. "No. Not that I know of."

Sara was unconvinced by Sasha's response. "She seemed happy in her relationship with her boyfriend?"

Sasha gasped. "Yes. Do you think he's hurt her?"

Sara sat back and folded her arms. "We're unsure what has happened to her right now. Is there a possibility of him harming her?"

"No, I don't think so. I don't really know Greg well but he doesn't seem the type to go around beating up women."

"That's reassuring for us to know. Thank you. How close are you to Amber?"

"Very close. We've been friends since primary school."

"Do you contact each other much?"

"Every da… umm, we used to ring each other every day. Less so nowadays."

Sara picked up on a sudden switch in direction in her words. "Have you fallen out lately, is that what you're telling me?"

"Oh, no. Nothing like that. It's just life getting in the way, I suppose. You know how it is, working full-time, going home knackered at the end of the day and not finding the time to socialise." Sasha said all this with her gaze fixed on the table once more.

Sara laughed. "Ain't that the truth? If it wasn't for my husband, there wouldn't be a meal on the table every evening, I'm always sapped of energy when I walk through my front door. I expect you're the same after being on your feet all day around here, right?"

"That's it, totally knackered most days, I can tell you."

"What about Amber, she works at Boots, yes?"

"Yes. She's the same, that's why we don't tend to go out much during the week."

"And at the weekends, she spends most of her time with Greg, right?"

"Sort of. Either that or catching up on sleep after her hectic week."

"So it's not uncommon for you to go weeks without either seeing or hearing from each other, is that what you're telling me?"

"Yes, that's it. Weeks at a time. It's a shame, we used to be really close."

"That is a pity, and that's only because of the pressures of work, not because you've fallen out with each other?" Sara repeated the question.

"Oh, no. She's my best friend. I love her like a sister."

Hmm… and yet you're not reacting like you're upset about her going missing. "Did you know that she was missing?"

"Yes, I think it was Greg who rang me to tell me."

Still, there was no eye contact. "Ah, I see. It must be upsetting for you."

"It is. I'm devastated by the news."

"Greg told us that he'd been out there searching for her, have you managed to join him in the search?"

Sasha swallowed. "No, I simply haven't had the time. The boss wanted me to work later last night. One of the girls is on maternity leave, and we're under pressure to get this stock out before the area manager shows up at the end of the week. I really shouldn't be taking the piss, sorry, mick, sitting around speaking to you all day."

"Of course. Well, I appreciate you spending the time with us. I'll leave you my card. Should you want to discuss anything further, just give me a call." She placed the card in front of Sasha.

The girl snatched it up and darted out of the room.

Sara and Craig stared at each other. "Well, that didn't go as expected, did it?" Sara stated.

"Mighty suspicious reactions to me. You think she knows where she is?"

Sara peered over her shoulder at the open door. "Something is amiss."

"Would it be worth putting her under surveillance?" Craig asked.

"You know what, I wouldn't ordinarily, but there's just something really off about the way she reacted to some of my questions that is twisting my gut. Let's get back to the station and get things organised."

"I don't mind volunteering. It seems like she'll be indisposed for a few hours around here."

"I agree. Come on, let's go."

Sara led the way back through the stockroom. Out of the corner of her eye, she spotted Sasha ripping open one of the boxes with force, spilling the contents on the floor and kicking out at the box, which only added to Sara's suspicions. Back in the shop, she thanked the woman who she'd first spoken to, and they made their way out to the car.

"I take it you noticed her reaction in the stockroom," Craig said.

"I did. A tad over the top. The more I think about it, the more sceptical I'm becoming. We have Amber's laptop, let's hope that gives us an indication of what's going on in her life, because let's face it, none of her family, her boyfriend or best friend appear to know. Or should I say, are unwilling to tell us, in some cases."

"That seems strange to me."

"Yep, none of it adds up at all. Either Amber has got in with the wrong crowd or... to be honest, I can't think of another scenario, especially after what we've just witnessed with Sasha."

"I'm inclined to agree with you."

Sara slipped into first gear and pulled out of the car park.

"Just thinking," Craig began moments later.

"Go on, it's good to bounce ideas around. What's on your mind?"

"We should be trying to trace her phone. See what activity there was before she went missing."

Sara pointed at him. "Excellent idea. I would have got around to suggesting the same thing soon enough. Make that your priority when we get back."

"Will do. Hopefully that will give us a direction to go in at least."

"The boyfriend and parents said they'd rung the number and it had gone into voicemail so it must still be active, yes?"

"Definitely. It's all too weird, isn't it?"

"Yep, taxing my wee brain cells, that's for sure. Hopefully things will start to make sense for us soon."

They reached the station and joined the rest of the team. After checking how Carla was and being told not to cluck like a mother hen by her partner, Sara brought the team up to date with what they'd discovered in the few hours out in the field.

"Are you telling me you think the best friend knows what's going on?" Carla tapped her pen on her cheek.

"It would seem that way. Craig suggested putting Sasha under surveillance, which I agree is the way to go. If only to satisfy our curiosity about her reaction to the news."

"I'll get on with obtaining Amber's phone records, see what that highlights, if anything," Craig announced.

"You do that. I'm going to get a press conference organised. Since speaking with Sasha, I have a bad feeling about this case. We need to get on top of it soon before it's too late for Amber and something bad happens to her."

"What do you want the rest of us to do?" Carla asked.

"We've already got a recent bank statement, courtesy of her parents, so there's no need to look at her financial background. Organising the surveillance team and possibly another team to go to her place of work, Boots, to interview her colleagues. Yes, I think we should do that ASAP. I'll leave you to deal with that, Carla. In the meantime, I'll get on to the press officer."

She dashed into her office and called Jane Donaldson. "Jane, sorry to trouble you, it's Sara Ramsey."

"Don't tell me, you need me to gather the press for an urgent conference. How urgent?"

"You know me too well. Any chance we can get it sorted for today? How are you fixed?"

"I have one already actioned for today, what I'll try to do is combine the two, if that's all right with you?"

"That would be brilliant. I can't thank you enough for this. We've got a missing teenager and the quicker we can get the word out, the better."

"Consider it done. Let me dot the i's and cross the t's and get back to you with a time."

"Amazeballs. Thanks, Jane, I knew I could rely on you."

"Pleasure as always. I'll be in touch soon, give me twenty minutes."

Sara ended the call and tried to break the back of her post while she waited.

A little while later, Jane confirmed the details as promised and told her she'd managed to slot her in after the other conference, which was scheduled to take place at three, with a five-minute interval in between. Sara was relieved to hear that. The sooner the word got out, the more likely they were to trace Amber.

She completed her morning chore, jotted down a few notes she wanted to use for the conference, then rejoined the team.

Her colleagues were all busy, heads down, doing her proud. She stopped by Carla's desk and asked the obligatory question.

Carla rolled her eyes. "Ask me if I'm all right one more time and I'll…"

Sara raised an eyebrow. "You'll do what? Bearing in mind I'm your superior officer."

"I know, but I also told you I didn't want you to make a fuss."

Sara held her hands up and backed away. "Can I buy you a coffee or would that be deemed as 'making a fuss'?"

Carla nodded. "A coffee would be a welcome distraction, thank you. You need a hand?"

"I'm buying them for everyone, so yes, thanks."

Sara bought the drinks while Carla distributed them.

Collecting her cup from Carla's desk, she announced that the press conference had been confirmed. "Okay, we need to organise a surveillance team to follow Sasha, any volunteers?"

Carla's hand was the first to shoot up in the air. "I'm going stir crazy around here already. I'd love the chance to do it."

"I'll tag along with Carla," Will volunteered.

Carla smiled at her partner and nodded. "Sounds a good idea to me."

"Hmm… are you sure you're up to it?"

"Definitely. Go on, boss. We'll only be following her, not getting into any altercations."

"All right then, if you're sure. Why don't you set off now?"

"Umm… one major question," Will started, "how are we going to know what she looks like?"

"Leave that to me. It's Sasha Minnow, right?" Carla tapped at her phone and showed an image of the young woman to Will. "Say hello to Sasha Minnow, courtesy of social media."

"Smartarse," Will mumbled.

Carla grinned.

Sara observed her partner, pleased that she appeared to be feeling much better after her ordeal.

"Come on then, time's getting on, Will." Carla got to her feet and hitched on her jacket. They left the incident room a few seconds later.

"She seems back to normal already," Craig observed.

"You can't keep a good woman down for long, Craig, many a man has tried in the past but failed." Sara chuckled. "Let's get back to it. I'm really not counting on you finding much this early in the investigation, that's why I took the decision to call the conference today instead of later on in the week. The sooner we get the word out there, the more chance we have of finding this young woman alive."

The team agreed and immersed themselves in their work. Sara did the rounds to check on their progress, which was minimal, until she reached Craig. He was buzzing with excitement. "What have you got, Craig?"

"I've managed to locate Amber's phone number, and her records have just come through."

Sara pulled up a chair next to him and studied the list with him. "Interesting, we've got a few consistent numbers here. I'm thinking they either belong to Greg or Sasha, possibly another close friend."

"I agree, I'll need to get their numbers to cross-check them. There's a number here, a one-off which she rang on Friday of last week."

Sara reached for the phone on the desk and dialled it. The number was dead. "Strange, nothing, no voicemail or anything, it just went dead. Let me try ringing Amber's number, or did you already ring it?"

"No, I didn't get the chance."

Sara dialled Amber's number, and it went into voicemail after several rings. "Well, that gives me hope the phone is still active."

"Maybe she has it hidden, if someone has abducted her. We could possibly set up a trace on it, just in case she comes back online."

"Good idea, I'll leave that in your capable hands. I'll be in my office, chasing up Forensics about the laptop. Give me a shout if you stumble across anything else."

"Yikes, good luck on that one."

"I know, I'm taking a risk ringing them early, but while there's a chance this girl is alive, I'll push them to the limit."

She slipped back into her office and called the lab. She mentally kicked herself for not getting the technician's name when they met earlier.

A male answered her call. She explained the situation, and he passed her over to another department.

"Ah, Inspector. This is James, we met a few hours ago."

"Hello, James. Sorry to bug you so soon, any news for me?"

"As it happens, I was just about to ring you."

"Sounds promising."

"I hope so. Looking at the emails on Miss Rowse's computer, it would appear that she applied for a job and was due to meet someone regarding an interview on Monday."

"Whoa! Okay, that's good news. Hang on, her parents never mentioned anything to me about this."

"Maybe they didn't know."

"Yep, that's a possibility. Perhaps she wanted to surprise them. Can you send me the email?"

"I can certainly do that, then you can judge for yourself."

"I appreciate it." She gave James her email address and hung up. Then, she booted up her computer and tapped her fingers until it pinged. Sara opened the email. It was from a Barrows Associates and signed by Henry Barrows. She quickly searched the internet for any business based in the Hereford area and came up blank. Sara decided to cast her net farther afield for the name of the business. Again, the result remained a negative one. She then input the name *Henry Barrows* but shook her head in disappointment at the zero return on that as well. "Damn and blast. I thought we were onto something there."

She left the office to inform the rest of the team and ask if they had any further suggestions. Jill nodded. "I could ring Companies House, see if the business is registered with them."

"Do that, thanks, Jill. I'm getting an ever-sinking feeling about this investigation."

3

"Have you fed her yet?" Harvey asked his twin brother.

"She's refusing to eat. Says she'd rather die than eat anything we have on offer."

Harvey shrugged. "Makes no odds to me. Let her starve. We'll have some fun with her in the meantime, though."

Daniel tutted. "Remind me why we are doing this again?"

"Are you for real?"

"It was a serious question. You think we're going to get away with it?"

"With my brains behind the operation, why not?"

"You're a sick shit. No idea why I decided to get dragged into this."

"Because you were bored, just like me. You better buck your ideas up, bro, because this is just the beginning."

"And what if I've changed my mind?"

Harvey inclined his head and glared at him. "Tough. You change your mind now, well… let's just say I have something on you that will persuade you every time. You'd be wise to remember that."

"Shit! You're always flinging that one at me. All that happened years ago, it's the biggest regret of my life. No, let me rephrase that.

My biggest regret is confiding in you, because since then, you've had a fucking hold over me."

"Now, brother dearest, you know that's not true. We've always shared our darkest secrets. We're partners, always have been. Linked by our time together in Mum's womb and rarely parted since we were born."

"Yeah, don't remind me."

Harvey playfully punched his brother in the arm. "Come on, it's time we had some fun with her."

"I can't do it."

"Do I have to force you?"

"You can try."

Harvey narrowed his eyes at his twin. "I'm warning you, don't go soft on me."

"And what if I said I wanted to forget this deal and walk away?"

Harvey shrugged. "I've already told you. I'm not in the habit of repeating myself. I'll see you later, I'm going to grab myself some free pussy."

He left his brother and went into the colder part of the house. This area was carved into the hillside, bare rock lining the walls instead of insulated plasterboard. On the single bed in the corner of the room sat his prey. She was pressed up against the stone wall, her arms clasped around her legs. She had bindings around her arms and one leg chained to the bedframe.

"Hello, Amber. I hear you're refusing to eat. Is that wise?" he asked in a sinister sing-song voice.

She shrank farther back into the wall, her face tear-stained, traces of mascara trailing down her cheeks. "Please, let me go. What do you want with me?" she whispered, her voice faltering and laden with terror.

Harvey approached the bed and sat on the end. He ran a finger up one of her shins. She flinched and recoiled from his touch. "Now, now, there's no need to be scared. If you do as I say, you won't get hurt. Are you going to do that?"

She shook her head and then nodded, the confusion evident in her watery eyes. "I don't want to be here, like this. I want to go home."

"I want to go home," he mimicked, his eyes boring into hers before lowering to take in her skinny body. "Why don't you try to persuade me to let you go?"

"I don't understand… how?"

He bared his stark white teeth in an expansive grin and placed a finger on his cheek. Tapping it, he said, "Let me think. Ah yes, I've got the answer. By spreading your legs for me."

"Never. I won't do it. You can't make me."

He swiped her across the face. "Hush, now. Don't you go telling me what I can and can't do. This is why you're going to need sustenance, to keep your strength up. I have a vigorous appetite that needs satisfying, if you get what I mean?"

She shook her head, he predicted more out of disbelief than misunderstanding his intentions. "I have a boyfriend. Please, I love him. I don't want anyone else."

"While it's admirable that you love him, can the same be said for him? We have your phone, do you think he's tried to contact you? No, he hasn't, so what does that tell you?"

"I don't believe you. Greg would never abandon me, if that's what you're suggesting."

"What, in your hour of need?" His head tipped back, and he laughed long and hard.

"Leave her alone, Harvey." Daniel appeared in the doorway.

He leapt off the bed and stormed over to his twin. Grabbing him around the throat, he pinned him up against the rock face. "Just because you've turned yellow all of a sudden doesn't give you the right to come in here, shouting the odds at me. I'm my own person. I do what I want, when I want to do it. Got that, dickhead?"

His brother gripped Harvey's hand, tried to remove it from his throat but Harvey squeezed tighter, cutting off Daniel's air supply. "Stop! Harvey, stop."

As if realising he'd possibly gone too far, Harvey relinquished his hold and backed up a couple of paces. "I refuse to apologise. You pushed me. You need to accept the situation for what it is, bro, or fuck off."

Daniel walked out of the room, and Harvey slammed the door shut behind him. He marched back over to where Amber was now trembling on the bed. He leaned down into her face and sneered. "See what you've made me do. I'm going to teach you a lesson you're not likely to forget now. I've had it with your whimpering pleas for help. They're pitiful and falling on deaf ears from now on. I'm warning you, fight me at your peril, bitch. Take what's coming to you, and I'll consider letting you go within a few days. If not... well, I'm sure you can figure that one out for yourself."

Amber gasped and sobbed. The fear intensified in her eyes, and her mouth fell open once he started removing his clothes. He stood in front of her, naked, his erection prominent with his intent. Shocked, her sobs echoed in the almost empty room, her gaze fixed to the wall beside her. He yanked her arm, forcing her to look at him.

Her bound hands shot up and covered her face. "No! I won't do it!"

"That's what you think." He slapped her again.

She let out a pitiful shriek as her head crashed against the wall.

He pulled her around to face him again. Blood trickled from a gash in her forehead. He traced the skin next to the trail of blood. "Why do it? Why fight the inevitable? You really want to do that? Give it up, you won't defeat me in my purpose. I will take what I want from you."

"No... no..."

He tore at her clothes, pulling the layers aside to gain access. The fabric pooled at her bound hands and feet.

She bucked like a determined mule and tried to kick out at him. Bored with her antics now, he did the only thing open to him. He punched her. Her head snapped to the side and settled against the wall. She was out cold.

He went to work, eager to satisfy the craving that had driven him to this extreme. *She shouldn't have fought. She's spoilt my fun, the fun of the chase and the jubilation of the capture. She's mine!*

. . .

*H*arvey rejoined his brother in the small kitchen around ten minutes later. Daniel was sitting at the table, his head in his hands.

"All right, bro?" Harvey squeezed his brother's shoulder on his way to the fridge. He removed a bottle of Chablis and opened it. He handed a glass to his brother. Daniel refused to accept it.

"I don't want one. How can you see this as some kind of celebration?"

"Get a life, Daniel. It *is* a celebration, I'll do it alone if necessary, no skin off my nose. You should have seen her in there, she gave as good as she got, if you get my drift."

"You disgust me."

"Says you, who…"

"Don't start. Leave it in the past."

"Where's the fun in that?" Harvey asked. He took a large gulp of wine and spun his glass around by the stem. "You're letting me down. I'm getting the impression you want to back out of the deal."

"You catch on slowly. Fucking hell, I can't believe it's only just sinking in."

"Cut the crap, Daniel. Climb down from your principled mountain and accept the situation for what it is."

"Why should I?"

Harvey heaved out a sigh. "Because if you don't, you can say farewell to any inheritance coming your way."

Daniel laughed. "You see, that's what I mean, you're frigging warped. Insane even."

"How do you figure that out?"

"What do you propose will happen when Mum and Dad find out about all of this shit? You think they'll slap us both on the back? Wrong with a capital W, mate."

Harvey fell silent. But only for a moment. "Well, with everything we have in place, the likelihood of that happening is non-existent. So, we'll be high and dry, ready to rock and roll when the time comes to hand her over."

"She doesn't deserve this, neither do the others."

"We've been over this a thousand times already. Give me a break and stop pulling against me. In order for us to succeed, we need to show a united front in all we do, and to be honest with you, I ain't getting that, not right now."

"I can't guarantee you will in the future, either."

Harvey noted the defeat in his brother's voice. "You're negating on our deal, is that what you're saying?" He yelled. "In spite of the warning I gave you barely half an hour ago. How do you think our folks are going to react when they find out what you did?"

"As if I care any more." Daniel shrugged. "It was nothing compared to what you have planned. For what? Money. Bloody money, that's all you care about. You should be putting yourself in their shoes." He pointed at the door. "How do you think these girls will feel when you abduct them and ship them out to the highest bidder? All to line your own pockets."

"Correction, *our* pockets." Harvey sighed impatiently. "This was a team effort, abducting her. It was you who flew the plane, or have you conveniently forgotten that part? I guess you must have, otherwise you wouldn't be giving me such grief. Your morals suck, I've told you that for years. Hence us embarking on this adventure. This financial venture which will probably make us millions and now, all of a sudden, you develop a conscience. You confuse the hell out of me." He downed his drink and tipped his chair over as he stood. "We need to get out of here. Get back to Hereford."

"We can't just leave her here, alone."

"Can't we?" He rushed forward and jabbed his brother in the chest. "Who says? Are you telling me you want to remain here with her?"

Daniel recoiled from his aggression. "Why not?"

Harvey slammed his clenched fist on the table and shouted in his brother's face, "It's not in the plan. The same blasted plan you agreed to partake in last month when we started all this."

"I'm allowed to change my mind. I'm a grown man."

"Except you're not... allowed to change your mind, that is. As for the grown man part, start bloody acting your age and not like a whining teenager."

"Sod off."

"I rest my case. You, big kid. Now, pack your bag, we're going tonight and don't even think about objecting to flying at night, or you'll get my fist in your face."

"I won't. Like I said already, you're a sick shit."

"Yep, I totally agree, and the best thing you can do to keep this 'sick shit' happy is to go along with the plan we agreed to work with."

Daniel rose from his chair and shrugged. He left the room and returned a few minutes later, carrying a rucksack.

"Don't tell me you didn't pack my bag as well."

"Fuck off! I ain't your slave. Do it yourself."

"I'll be right back." He kicked out at the chair leg. "I can't wait to get out of this dump and back to Hereford. I never thought I'd hear myself saying that."

4
_____

Sara paced the hallway outside the appointed press conference room; the previous inspector was running late, eating into her slot. She wasn't happy, she hated dealing with the press as a rule, without the added stress of pacing the corridor until one of her colleagues had finished their appeal.

The door flew open and DI David Cooper exited the room, his cheeks resembling an over-ripe tomato. "God, I hate it. My apologies for holding you up, Sara. The savages wouldn't stop firing questions at me, most of them useless, I hasten to add."

"Not to worry, at least you made it out of there alive."

"Barely." He wiped the beads of sweat from his brow and then ran up the concrete stairs next to her.

Jane emerged from the room moments later. "Are you good to go?"

"I am. Ready to tear into me, are they?"

Jane chuckled. "Some of them might. They're eager to leave, so we'd better get in there quickly while there's a glimmer of hope of keeping their interest."

Sara's eyes widened. "Are you kidding me? As if I'm not nervous enough already, you have to fling that into the mix."

Jane reached for her arm, turned and headed back into the room, tugging Sara behind her. "You worry too much and sometimes forget that I'm here to hold your hand. Just say your piece to the cameras. I'll limit the questions, it's not as if you can give them any other titbits this early on in the investigation, is it?"

"No, that's right. Okay, I feel a bit better now. You can unhitch my arm, Jane."

"Sorry, force of habit. Let's get this show on the road."

Sara sat next to Jane on the mini stage, a sea of pissed-off faces watching their every movement. After Jane introduced her to the crowd, Sara cleared her throat and began.

She told the press the reason they were there, then looked directly into the television camera a few feet in front of her to present her plea to the public. "If anyone saw this young woman, Amber Rowse, on Monday, the day she went missing, or indeed any day since then, please contact me on the number at the bottom of your screen. I can't emphasise enough the importance of finding Amber quickly. Any questions?"

One of the male journalists raised his right hand. "Why the importance in finding her early, apart from the obvious? Is she ill? Does she have ongoing health issues?"

"Not that I'm aware of, no. In any missing person case, it's always imperative we find the person promptly."

The journalist nodded, seemingly satisfied with her response, and then asked, "What do you believe has happened to her?"

"It's really too early to speculate. In fact, I'd rather steer clear of any kind of supposition and stick to the facts. We have a nineteen-year-old woman missing, something that is completely out of character for her. If you've seen Amber recently, please contact me. Amber, if you're watching this, please come home, your parents miss you terribly and are worried sick about you."

A few more journalists raised their hands to ask the obscurest of questions, which Sara batted away. She drew the conference to a close and left the room with Jane.

Outside, before the journalists came out, Sara let out the breath she'd been holding in. "Gosh, I hate dealing with the press regarding missing person cases."

"I know what you mean. The journos definitely act differently."

"Yeah, glad I'm not the only one who thinks that. Right, I'm going to shoot upstairs and wait for all the dozens of calls to come in."

Jane held up her crossed fingers. "Here's hoping. Can you let me know what happens with the girl? This one has really hit a nerve for some reason."

"Probably because you've got a teenage daughter of your own, Jane."

"You're right. I intend to sit her down tonight, force her to listen to the plea and have a chat with her about her own safety. There are far too many cases of this nature hitting the headlines at present. The last thing I want is for her to become a statistic."

"Try not to worry unduly. If you've never needed to be concerned about your daughter before, scare tactics might have the reverse effect. Maybe watch the plea with her and ask her what she thinks and go from there."

"You're a wise woman, Sara Ramsey. Why didn't I think of that?"

Sara grinned. "Not bad for a novice who doesn't have kids, right?" Sara laughed and ran up the stairs, into the incident room. "I'm in dire need of a caffeine fix."

Jill beat her to it and leapt out of her chair and rushed towards the vending machine. "Don't say I never put my hand in my pocket." She laughed and handed Sara the cup of coffee.

"I wouldn't dream of it. How are things looking?"

"Slow and laborious. How did the conference go?"

Sara shrugged. "It was okay. We'll see where it leads."

"Are you hopeful? What if nothing comes of it?"

"Don't say that, and no, I'm not hopeful. However, I think we should remain positive, don't you? I'm not willing to give up on Amber just yet."

"Nor should we. I just wondered what our chances were of finding this girl alive. There, I've said it."

"It's a tough call, Jill. But we must remain upbeat about things otherwise, you know as well as I do, where a slippery slope can lead us. Now, what have you found out?"

Jill tumbled into her chair and held up a few pieces of paper. "I'm in the process of checking out several aspects at the same time. Unfortunately, nothing has come back on anything yet. Sorry to disappoint you."

Sara picked up a pen and tapped it thoughtfully. "You haven't. I appreciate it's early days, even if I am getting antsy about things. All I want to know is whether Amber is safe and well somewhere. That's not much to ask, is it?"

"No, not at all. After speaking with her boyfriend and parents, what is the likelihood of her just taking off?"

She dropped her pen and shook her head. "Not on the agenda, not for me. Surely, if her intention was to take off, she'd be in a better state financially and would have packed a bag, wouldn't she?"

"Possibly. What if she met another fella who has promised her the earth and told her to leave everything behind and go away with him?"

Sara laughed. "There's a possibility, but highly unlikely. That type of thing only ever happens in the pages of a romance novel, doesn't it? I'm going to touch base with Carla and Will, see if they've got any news for us yet." She went into her office and picked up the phone. "Carla, any news?"

"Nothing so far. We're parked up outside the rear entrance of New Look, no one has come or gone since we arrived. How did the conference go?"

"It went. Not sure how fruitful it's going to prove to be, I don't suppose we'll know until later." Sara glanced at her watch. "It's almost four-thirty now, I'm presuming New Look closes its doors around five-thirty. Therefore, kicking out time should happen not long after. Let me know when she leaves, if you would?"

"Sure thing. What about manning the phones tonight?"

"I'm going to do that myself. Just going to ring Mark to warn him I'll be late."

"Okay. I'll be in touch soon, I hope."

Sara pressed the End Call button and immediately rang her

husband. She trawled her mind, trying to recall if he'd mentioned whether he had any operations on today or not. She couldn't think of any such conversation. "Hi, am I disturbing you?"

"You never disturb me. What's up?"

"Apart from wanting to hear your voice, nothing much... except that I might be working late tonight."

"That's a shame. I'd planned something special for dinner, nothing that can't wait though, before your guilt gene starts spiking."

"You really do know me so well. Sorry, love, we're dealing with an important case, and I've put out a call through the media today for the public's help."

"I trust you, Sara, you don't have to make excuses."

"I wasn't, I promise."

"Any leads on the case?"

"Nothing much so far. We've got a nineteen-year-old girl who has been reported missing by her parents."

"Oh, Christ, when?"

"On Monday."

"Ugh... is there a reason for the delay? If my daughter went missing, I'd be down the cop shop the very next day."

"I hear you. The parents work opposite shifts and neither of them realised she'd gone. That's it in a nutshell, but I think there's more to it than that, judging by the conversation I had with the girl's best friend."

"Sounds ominous."

"Maybe. I've got the friend under surveillance, just in case. Anyway, how are things there? Any new wee or pooh stains on your uniform today?"

He snorted. "Every single day. Luckily, they're from a litter of puppies this time."

"Oh, don't tell me they were dumped."

"No, it was a caesarean birth. They're adorable. All the nurses are going gaga over them."

"So cute. Okay, I must fly. Sending my love, I'll keep you up to date about when to expect me."

"Don't work too hard. Not that you're likely to listen to me."

"I always listen to you, my darling husband."

"Can you say that with less sarcasm next time?"

Sara laughed. "You're nuts. I'm going now. Love you."

"Ditto. See you later."

*T*he rest of the team drifted off at around sixish, leaving Sara to man the phones. The first thing she did was contact Carla and Will. "Any news yet?"

"Yes, sorry, she left work at five-forty-five. We've followed her at a snail's pace. She jumped on a bus and is now on foot; I'm guessing she's on her way home."

"What's her demeanour like?"

"When her head isn't down, she's mostly looking over her shoulder, acting suspicious."

"Suspicious or nervous?" Sara asked.

"Maybe the latter. You think she's worried she's going to be abducted?"

"Possibly, it would make sense. We got the phone records back. Amber rang a regular number, I'm taking a punt she was calling Sasha. We'll go over it properly, matching times *et cetera* with Sasha's statement and yank her in, if we have to, for more questioning."

"Sounds like a plan. What do you want us to do tonight?"

"See if she goes home, or ends up somewhere else and then call it a day. I think her mannerisms are speaking volumes at this moment."

"Are you still at work?"

"Yep, manning the phones. I'm hopeful we'll get a response, we'll see."

"I'll drop in and see you before heading home."

"Okay, see you later."

The local evening news aired at six. Sara watched the conference go out at around six-twenty and sat by the phone, willing it to ring. Twenty minutes later, two phone calls came in within minutes of each other. One was an obvious time-waster, a young bloke who gave her false information who then laughed and hung up, leaving her seething. The second call was from a gentleman which sparked her interest.

"Hello, sir, can I take your name for our records?"

"Yes, it's Alan Baldwin."

"And why are you calling this evening, sir?" Sara poised her pen ready to take down what he had to tell her, if anything.

"I saw her. The girl you're searching for."

"You did? When? Where?"

"She was on the bus, she got off near the precinct."

"Can you recall what time this was?"

"Around ten-thirty, Monday morning. I was sat behind her on the bus. She was on the phone, I overheard parts of her conversation, she mentioned being nervous."

Sara scribbled down the information, her scrawl in a race with the adrenaline that was pumping around her system. "Nervous? Any idea why?"

"I wasn't eavesdropping, I promise. She was talking loudly, the bus was noisy, you see, she was trying to be heard above the din. Anyway, from what I could tell, she was on her way to an interview. That's all I managed to pick up."

"That's brilliant, no need to apologise, I'm glad you called us this evening. This will give us a new lead to chase up. Going back to the phone call, do you know who it was to? Did you hear any names mentioned?"

"Let me think, I'm not usually good with names. I think she did mention one... now then, what was it?" he paused to think and sighed. "No, it's escaped my mind. Now I feel like I've let you down."

"You mustn't think like that. You've given us something new to sink our teeth into. Did you get the impression she was speaking to someone she knew well?"

"Oh, yes, I would say someone like a best friend, something along those lines. I don't think it sounded as though she was talking to a parent. Don't ask how I know that."

"I understand. Are you telling me her tone was more natural than stilted, perhaps?"

"Yes, yes. That's it."

"And you say she got off at the precinct?"

"That's right. She was also dressed smartly, if that helps?"

"It does. Did you notice which direction she went in?"

"Towards the main shopping area. She seemed in a hurry."

"Hmm… so the interview would have likely taken place in the centre of the city, then." Sara muttered the assumption more to herself than to Mr Baldwin.

"Possibly. She didn't get on any other form of transport, anyway."

"Thanks so much for your call. Was there anything else you can think of?"

"No, I believe that's all. I hope you find her. I'll be sending out a prayer for God to keep her safe in the meantime."

"Thank you. I'm sure her parents will appreciate your thoughtfulness, sir."

"Goodnight, Inspector."

"Goodnight." She ended the call and jotted down the information Mr Baldwin had given her on the whiteboard. She stood back and assessed what she'd written, but her line of thinking was interrupted by the telephone ringing again. She shot across the room to answer it. "DI Sara Ramsey, how may I help?"

"Hello, are you the person in charge of the missing girl case? Sorry, I've forgotten her name already. I just saw the clip on the news."

"I am. May I take your name?"

"It's Davina Harding. I think I saw her."

"You did? That's excellent news, may I ask where?"

"It was near the precinct on Monday. I'm a mobile hairdresser, you see. I was in the area, I have a client in town, she was desperate for a cut and colour… sorry, I've gone off track, haven't I?"

Sara sniggered. "Just a little. What can you tell me about Amber Rowse?"

"Ah yes, that's her name, I knew it was something weird or should I say uncommon. Anyway, I came away from Mrs Montgomery's at around half-tenish, she had an appointment with her gynaecologist at eleven hence the reason she wanted her hair doing so urgently. Oops…

here I go again… I saw the girl, thought how well-dressed she looked. I wasn't surprised when she got into one of those fancy cars."

"Wait, you saw her get into a vehicle?"

"That's what I said, didn't I? One of those long ones."

"Long one, as in a limousine?"

"That's the one. Sorry, my brain tends to go to mush in the evenings."

"No problem. I don't suppose you got the registration number, did you?"

Davina tutted. "You're right, I didn't. Had I known that she would step into the car and be reported missing a few days later, then maybe I would've taken more notice. Sorry."

"No need to apologise, that's a logical deduction. Did the car stay where it was or drive away?"

"She got in and it took off. Don't ask me where to, I'm not psychic. Sorry, that was uncalled for, you didn't deserve that retort."

"We agree on one thing." Sara chuckled. "Did you see the driver of the vehicle or were the windows blacked out?"

"Yes, they were, but the chauffeur got out of the car to open the door for the young woman."

"I see. Can you tell me what her reaction was?"

"She seemed embarrassed, I thought that was odd. But there was no reluctance to get into the car, not from where I was standing."

"And the car left soon after?"

"Yes. I watched it drive off, it was as if I was mesmerised by the whole scene. I shook myself out of my state and walked off towards Tesco's to pick up my car."

"I suppose it's not every day you see a limo in the centre of the city like that."

"It was a first for me, I can tell you. I hope I've helped a smidge. Poor girl must be frantic, going out of her mind with worry."

"I would suggest the same, which was why I called a press conference early. I truly appreciate you getting in touch. What you've given me could turn out to be really important."

"You think? I hope so. I try to help the police when I can. I called your lot out to my estate when four lads were kicking a cat around like a football at the park at the end of my road. I tried to stop them, but they gave me a right mouthful. Your lot arrived within minutes, thank goodness. Turns out it was my neighbour's cat. Poor thing was so badly injured that she had to be put to sleep, the vet couldn't save her. Brain damaged it was. Bloody kids of today need a good thrashing, I'd volunteer to do that if I could."

"That's terrible. I recall the case. My husband is a vet, I remember him saying at the time he thought the cat wouldn't survive. Anyway, thanks for taking the time to call in tonight, it means a lot."

"You're welcome. Please do what you can to find her, she seemed such a nice girl from a distance."

"I will, I promise. If you hadn't rung this evening, my job would have been a whole lot harder. Thank you again."

Carla and Will stepped into the room as she ended the call. "Good news, guys. I'll tell you about it over a coffee."

"I'll get them," Will volunteered.

"Thanks, I knew you were my favourite for a reason, Will. I take it Sasha went straight home?"

Carla eased herself into the chair next to Sara. "She did. Here, I took a video of her movements. The closer she got to her home, the more agitated she became."

Sara watched the young woman constantly peering over her shoulder and up her pace now and again. "Yep, she seems dead nervous to me."

Will deposited two cups on the desk for her and Carla. He cleared his throat and shuffled his feet a little.

"Spit it out, Will," Sara demanded. She noticed he'd only bought the two cups of coffee.

"I was wondering if it would be all right if I shot off, boss. I promised my mates I'd meet them for a game of snooker tonight."

"One sec, I'd like a brief chat in my office, if that's okay?"

They entered the office and Sara closed the door. "I know you've been with Carla most of the afternoon, but did you manage to do any research on her possible attacker before you went?"

"I did. I checked back over the recent cases, and well, to be honest with you, it's like looking for a needle in a haystack, boss. All the cases we've solved in the past six months, any one of those bastards could be responsible."

Sara growled. "Not what I wanted to hear. This case has to take priority now, we'll revisit Carla's attacker afterwards. Saying that, if things should go quiet around here, will you promise me you'll do some more digging on the hush hush?"

"Of course. I still reckon someone should pay her ex a visit. Too much of a coincidence to me."

"Yeah, maybe I'll drop round and have a quick word with him. All right, get out of here. You've done your stint for the day. Thanks for taking care of Carla today."

"Always a pleasure having a pretty colleague sharing the car with me instead of Barry." He grinned and sprinted out of the room.

"He's an odd one," Carla noted, once they were alone. "Barely said a word to me in the car, lost in his own thoughts most of the afternoon."

"Not fun for you, ever the chatterbox."

Carla groaned. "Bloody cheek, I am not."

Sara inclined her head and raised an eyebrow. "If you say so. Right, back to business. I've only had three calls, one was a time-waster, the other two are what I'd call golden ones."

"Sounds promising." Carla took a sip from her cup and motioned at the sheets of paper Sara was holding.

"We're going to need Craig to work his magic on the CCTV footage in the morning. So far, we have a gentleman who sat behind Amber on the bus. He told me she had a conversation with what sounded like a friend. Going for an interview was mentioned. Then, we have a hairdresser who saw Amber a little while later getting into a limousine."

"A what? Bloody hell. Who the fuck goes to an interview and gets picked up by a limousine?"

"Exactly, it's way out there in the realms of bizarre, if you ask me."

Carla shook her head. "Hard to believe. What are we looking at here, Sara? It doesn't bode well, does it?"

"Unless we find out what the interview was for, we're unlikely to find her."

"Do you want to pull Sasha in for questioning?"

"I'm moving in that direction. I think we should verify what we've been told first, then pull her in. I have an inkling she knows more than she's letting on."

"Looking at the footage I showed you, do you reckon she was nervous or terrified?" Carla asked.

"Hard to tell. Do you think she knows who has her and is terrified they'll come after her next?"

Carla sighed and shrugged. "It seems to be the only logical explanation."

"We need to match up the phone numbers and take another look at what Sasha told me. Either way, I'm not getting a good feeling about this. Maybe Sasha is in on it. Perhaps she arranged for someone to abduct her friend... no, that can't be right, she wouldn't be reacting like this if that was the case, would she?"

Carla pinched her forehead and flinched. "God knows. I'm too exhausted to try and figure it out."

Sara bashed her fist on the desk. "That's it. We'll call it a day and hit the ground hard in the morning."

"Are you sure?"

"Yep. The phones have gone dead now, anyway. Come on, let's both go home and get some rest. Do you want me to drop you off? Do you even want to go home? Jeff said he and Wendy could put you up. How are your aches and pains?"

"It's so kind of you all. No fussing, remember?"

"I'm not. I'm allowed to be concerned for a friend, aren't I?"

"I suppose. I'll be fine, as long as I sleep well tonight."

"You have your own concerns to worry about. We should start investigating the attack on you too, Carla."

"I'm fine. Don't worry about me."

"But I do."

"Then, stop. Are you ready to go?"

"Ah, the expert on changing the subject strikes again."

They left the incident room, Sara switched off the lights and closed the door behind them. In the car park, she again asked Carla if she was okay to drive home. Carla ignored her and got in her car and left before Sara had even had the chance to unlock hers.

She drove home, her thoughts on the case in hand, *Smooth Radio* playing softly in the background. She found Mark standing on the doorstep when she pulled into their road.

"Hello, you. Did you have a good day?" He kissed her and removed her coat.

She slipped off her shoes and reached out for a cuddle. "Yes and no. I'll tell you about it while we prepare dinner. How about you?"

"I got off lightly today, only a few bites from a frustrated parrot to add to my scars. Dinner is ready."

"Poor you. Wow, what are you about to delight me with tonight?"

"Gammon, pineapple, chips, tomatoes, mushrooms and sweetcorn."

"Crikey, sounds delicious. Do I have time to get changed?"

"Nope, I'm about to dish up."

"Oh well, no big deal. Can we have a bottle of wine or is that too much to ask, what with it being mid-week?"

"Go on, then. I'll leave that for you to do. I'll be busy serving up."

They entered the kitchen, and the smell sent her into a happy place for some reason. She removed two glasses from the cupboard next to the cooker and opened a bottle of Sauvignon Blanc.

They tucked into their meal, both apparently hungrier than they first thought. Halfway through, she decided to tell Mark about how the day had begun.

Mark's features were filled with worry for her colleague. "What? Who could possibly be responsible for doing that to poor Carla? Was she badly injured?"

"We've yet to determine that. I have my suspicions it might be Gary, but I wouldn't voice that openly, not to Carla."

"Hard to believe a fireman would go to such lengths as to punish his ex in that way."

"It's hard to believe anyone would, but the truth is, they did. Carla could barely move at work. She made my piss boil when she refused to go to the hospital, so, rather than let her sit there in agony, not knowing if she had a few broken bones or not, I got Jeff to call the duty doctor." Mark topped up their wine glasses and she took a sip before she continued, "She wasn't too happy about it, but tough. She needed to be examined. You should have seen her, black and blue all over, I'm presuming all over. Her face was discoloured, so much so that I refused to take her out with me today."

Mark winced. "Ouch, I bet that went down well."

"She admitted it was right for her to stay at the station, but come mid-afternoon, she was bored out of her mind. So, she volunteered to go on surveillance with Will."

"Bless her. It's tough sitting behind a desk once you've had the freedom to go out and about every day with the boss. Must have come as a shock to her system."

Sara sipped at her wine. "Yep. Anyway, we'll see how she is tomorrow and decide whether she can team up with me again or not. Thanks for a lovely dinner, sorry I was delayed getting home this evening."

"I saw the appeal go out. Was it prosperous?"

Sara dropped her knife on the plate and waved her flattened hand from side to side. "We'll find out in the morning. I felt bad coming away from the station so early, but there's little more we could have done tonight, anyway. I switched the phones over to the main call centre to handle. We'll sift through any extra calls that come in tomorrow."

"What's your gut saying about the case?"

"I have a few lingering doubts as to why a young woman would arrange an interview with someone in the back of a limousine, and why she felt the need to hide the impending interview from her parents. At least, I think she did, I'm assuming they would have mentioned it otherwise."

"It does sound strange." He pushed his empty plate away and leaned back. "I couldn't do your job. The fact you have to sift through minor evidence and assemble a case I'd find bewildering and yet you manage to successfully do it day in, day out."

"I've never really thought about it that way before. It's my job, you slip into a routine. Identify when to probe and when to hang back to see what develops."

"As in the case of the best friend, is that what you're getting at?"

"Exactly. We need to drag her into the station, screaming and kicking if necessary, to find out what she knows."

"Hard to believe she could be involved in her friend's disappearance."

"Involved? The jury is still out on that one. Possibly, being coerced into giving us a false statement. Either way, I'm determined to get to the damn truth and quickly. Amber's life is at risk."

"Why the limousine? What's the significance of that?"

"Maybe the person needed to entice her into thinking he was wealthy. Again, without knowing what type of job the interview was for, it's hard to say. Enough about work, I've had my share for the day. Let's get cleared up, correction, I'll clear up while you find something decent on the TV to watch tonight."

"I won't argue. Don't forget you promised to ring your mother back tonight."

"Yikes, thanks for the reminder, I had forgotten."

Mark helped her clear the table, kissed her and then went into the lounge. She FaceTimed her mother and angled the phone against the orchid plant sitting on the windowsill in front of her.

"Hi, Mum, I'm doing the washing-up, so forgive all the clattering of plates et cetera. How are you?"

"I'm fine. Your father had a rough day today. I've just put him to bed."

"Damn, what's wrong? Is it his heart again?"

"No, he couldn't tell me what was wrong. He's got a fever, hot and sticky. I gave him a couple of paracetamols. I'll check on him in a moment, I think he'll be asleep soon enough."

"Send him my love and wish him a speedy recovery."

"I'll do that. Now, you're not to worry about him, he's in safe hands."

"I know. Give us a shout if he gets any worse though, Mum."

"I will. Your sister is here, she's going to be staying with us a few days, so there really isn't any need for you to worry. How's work? Wait, before you answer that, we all watched you on TV this evening. Any news on the missing girl?"

"No, well, that's not quite true. We had a few useful calls come in, so we're hopeful of finding her soon."

"That is good news, dear. Okay, I'm glad you called. As you know, it's your father's birthday next weekend. I want to make this year a special occasion after... losing your brother. Will you and Mark join us for a celebratory meal on the Saturday?"

"That would be lovely, Mum. Do you need me to help with the catering or arrangements?"

"No, you have enough on your plate. Lesley is here to help with the finer details. It'll only be the immediate family."

"Sounds ideal. Dad's in the dark I take it?"

"Yes, at the moment, not sure how long it'll remain that way, but we're going to do our best."

"What about presents, what shall I get him this year?"

"Goodness, I don't know. Don't you think I have enough going on in my head without thinking about what present to buy him?"

"Sorry. I'll give him a fishing tackle voucher. Docklow Pools have a shop, I could nip out there next week or maybe I'll give them a call."

"How thoughtful. He'll love that. Okay, I'm going to let you get on with your evening now. I want to do some planning while he's out of the way."

"Good luck. Let me know by text how he is in the morning, if you would?"

"I'll do that. Love you, dear. Send Mark my love."

"I will. Love you, too."

5

---

*S*ara busied herself in her office with mundane paperwork until the team arrived. Carla poked her head into the room at five minutes to nine.

"We're all here now."

"How are you today? And no, that's not me being a fusspot." She smiled, doing her best to ward off another rebuke.

"A lot better. Thanks. The bruising seems to have gone down well overnight." She angled her face in different directions as if to emphasise her point.

Sara narrowed her eyes. "It's amazing what a little extra make-up will hide, right?"

Carla's grin carried a touch of sarcasm to it. "Don't know what you mean. Can I partner you today?"

Sara left her desk and joined Carla at the door. "I'll have to think about it." She paused and posed as Rodin's *Thinker* for a second or two. "All right, I've thunk. I don't see why not."

Carla spun on her heel and punched the air. Sara was relieved her partner had taken the news so well, nothing worse than spending a tough day at work with a mardy colleague.

She clapped to gain the team's attention. "Okay, I want to make this brief. We have a lot of angles we need to hit this morning." She went over the two calls she'd personally received from the appeal the night before and then sifted through the half dozen others that had come in after she'd left for the evening. There was no new evidence from what she could tell. "So, Craig, this morning, I need you to obtain the CCTV footage from Monday, specifically around the bus stop and in the precinct, if you will?"

He nodded. "Want me to try and get the footage from the bus as well?"

"Good idea. If you need a hand, give Barry a shout. Carla and I will be going over Amber's phone statement. There's also the matter of the firm in the email, we need to keep looking into that aspect. Anything else that I might have forgotten?"

"Would it be worth trying to find out how many limousines are in the area?" Jill suggested.

"Yes, although we don't have a registration number yet, not until Craig has scrolled through the footage, it might be good to make a start, Jill."

"What about trying to track Amber's phone?" Will asked.

Sara shrugged. "I wish there was a way. We can't do that until it's switched back on again. Worth a shout though, Will. Carla and I will be paying Sasha another visit this morning, now we have indisputable proof that we believe she contacted Amber on Monday and not Sunday. Why did she lie? Anything else, or is that enough to be going on with?"

"I think we've covered everything," Carla noted.

"Good. Right, are you ready, partner?"

"Too right. I can't wait to confront the little minx."

They left the incident room and wound their way down the concrete stairs. "Not sure I want to go in there to intentionally confront her. Let's play it casual for now, see if she slips up once she sees the evidence against her."

"Are you intending to question her at the shop or are you going to ask her to accompany us to the station?"

"I think the latter will have more impact, however, given the way she was reacting yesterday, maybe being hauled into the station will freak her out."

"Perhaps you're right. Either way, I'm eager to hear what she has to say or what excuse she's going to give for trying to deceive us."

They pulled into the staff car park at New Look five minutes later and entered the main entrance. The same assistant Sara spoke to the previous day was behind the counter. "Oh, hello again. Back so soon?"

"Yes. We have a few things we need to clear up with Sasha, if that's okay, is she around?"

"Nope. She called in sick this morning. I was livid, she knows we're all up against it around here with the area manager arriving any day for his annual inspection, and she drops me in it like this."

"Did she say what's wrong with her?" Sara asked, a nugget of concern tugging at her insides.

"No, apart from having flu-like symptoms. Astounding, considering she seemed to be fit and well enough yesterday. C'est la vie, we just have to accept it and move on."

"Sorry to hear that she's let you down. We'll drop over and see her."

"Ha... if she's there and not off out somewhere, gallivanting."

Sara smiled and nudged Carla to leave. "Thanks for your help."

They left the shop before either of them spoke again. "Hell, I hope she's okay. Maybe Will and I should have stuck around outside her house a bit longer last night, instead of calling it a day early."

"Don't go getting yourself all worked up. She could be genuinely ill. We'll know soon enough. Come on."

Sasha appeared devastated to see them standing on her doorstep when they rang the bell. She stepped back and allowed them to enter the hallway and whispered, "Do you mind keeping this down, Mum's not too well, hence the reason I rang in sick today."

"So, you haven't got the flu, then?"

"No. My boss is an ogre, she wouldn't have allowed me to have had the time off if I'd told her I needed it to care for Mum."

"I see. Can we go somewhere else to have a chat? Somewhere we're not likely to disturb your mother."

"Yes, come through to the kitchen, you'll have to excuse the mess. I'm trying to organise dinner for later. Mum said not to bother, but I wanted to make an effort for her, especially as she's not very well."

"May I ask what's wrong?" Sara asked once they'd entered the kitchen and closed the door behind them.

"She has fits, she's epileptic. I have to monitor her. Some days are worse than others."

"Is your mum married?"

"No, Dad left as soon as her epilepsy started to get worse."

"Sorry to hear that, Sasha."

"We cope, most of the time. I feel guilty leaving her and going to work every day, but if I stayed at home, there's no way we'd cope on benefits; Dad refuses to dip his hand in his pocket to send us any extra to cover the household expenses."

"That's such a shame."

"You're not here to offer me sympathy, we don't need it anyway. What's wrong, have you found Amber?"

Sara noticed a glimmer of hope enter the young woman's eyes. "Why don't we take a seat?"

They all sat around the circular pine table. Sasha reached for the salt pot and began twisting it nervously. "It's bad news, isn't it? She's not... dead, is she?"

"No, it's nothing like that, I promise. We simply need to review a few things you mentioned to me yesterday."

"Oh, such as?"

Sara withdrew the sheet of phone records, unfurled it and pressed it flat onto the table. "Maybe you can clarify your phone number for us, if you would?"

"I don't understand. Why? What's that?"

"This is Amber's latest phone record. What's your number, Sasha?"

Sasha closed her eyes for an instant as if she was regretting getting caught out and reeled off her number.

Sara tapped the paper at the bottom. "Your number is the last one she called."

"It was? Oh right, not surprising, we're very close. She's like the sister I've never had."

"I see. Now, this is the part that I find perplexing…"

Sasha's gaze darted between Sara and Carla. She let out a huge sigh, and her head flopped forward. "Am I in trouble?"

"For what? Making a false declaration? Did you, Sasha?"

Tears bulged and slipped onto her crimson cheeks. "I'm so sorry, it's just that… umm… they warned me not to say anything."

"They? Who are *they*?"

"The people who have Amber. They warned me that if I said anything to the police… oh God, I can't tell you anything else… they'll make good on their threat and kill her."

"It's pointless not telling us everything now. If you confide in us, there's every chance we can save Amber, but you're going to have to trust us."

"But… I can't. Please, don't force me. I want her to stay safe. If I open my mouth, she'll *die*."

"I understand what a horrendous predicament you're in, Sasha, but you need to do the right thing and tell us what you know."

"They could be here, watching my house. What if they are and they saw you turn up?" She covered her face with her hands and sobbed.

Sara rubbed her right arm. "That's it, get it all out. We checked, there was no one hanging around outside when we arrived, love." Sara cringed at how easily the lie slipped out of her mouth. She would say just about anything to get Sasha onside, in the hope that she revealed what they were likely up against.

Sasha shook her head. "I'm petrified of what they'll do. They threatened they would kill her and come back to get me. That's the truth, the reason I haven't stepped foot outside the door today. My mum isn't ill in bed, she's at work. Please, I didn't mean to deceive you. Don't punish me for trying to keep myself and my family safe."

Sara gripped Sasha's hand. "We can help to keep you safe, if you'll tell us what you know."

"That's just it, I don't really know much, except that Amber was due to meet a man for an interview and went missing. I spoke to her on Monday morning, she was on the bus on her way to meet this man. I told her to ring me after the interview, to let me know how she got on."

"And did she?" Sara glanced down to corroborate what she was thinking. "Yes, she called you at around three on Monday."

"No, she didn't. It wasn't her. It was an evil man. He told me that if I ever wanted to see her alive again, I was to tell the police that I hadn't spoken to Amber since Sunday."

"Did he say what his aim is? Why he's holding her?"

"No. The alarm bells should have rung long before she ever went for that damn interview."

"I don't understand. Why?"

"Who in their right mind employs a nineteen-year-old to be a globe-trotting assistant on a huge wage?"

"Is that what the job entailed?"

"Yes, she would have the world at her feet. Travel extensively, accompanying this man on business trips around the globe."

"What's his name, Sasha?"

She swallowed. "I don't know. I tried to get more information out of her, but for some reason she wanted to keep everything else a secret from me. Maybe he warned her not to spout her mouth off. I don't know. Jesus, I lay awake at night, regretting so much. Why didn't I try harder to persuade her that this job seemed too damn good to be true? I had my doubts about it, but she was so damned excited. I didn't want to press the point home and burst her bubble of euphoria. Oh God, now, I don't know what's going to happen to her. I'm distraught. I want her back, you have to help me save her."

"We're going to do our best. We'll arrange a safe house for you. This man, or these people, won't be able to find you, I promise."

"What if they ring me? They have her phone." She gasped. "Can't you trace it? You must be able to do that, surely?"

"Not at present, we've tried. The phone is turned off. Will you work with us?"

"If I have your assurance that my family and I will be safe."

"You do."

"Okay, but I really don't know much."

"How did Amber hear about the job vacancy?" Sara asked.

Carla opened up her notebook, ready to jot down the answers.

"Damn, she didn't say, and I didn't ask. How dumb is that of me? I should've bloody asked her. She was so excited. I didn't want my reservations to dampen her spirits. Amber loves money, spending it mostly. She saw the position as giving her a great start in life."

"We're aware that she has a fondness for shopping."

"I kept asking her where she got her money from. She had a new bag every bloody week, and she didn't buy them from the market either. I'm talking designer handbags that cost a packet."

"We found a bank statement in her room, she's in a lot of debt."

Sasha shook her head. "Why am I not surprised?"

"You believe she got a taste for the high life and sought out a specific role to apply for?"

"Maybe. She was very secretive in that respect. I'm sorry I can't tell you more."

"The name of the person who was interviewing her, perhaps?"

"Nope, sorry. It's not coming to me."

"If I mentioned the name Barrows Associates or Henry?"

"No, why? Is that the firm and the name of the person who she had the interview with?"

"We believe so, we found an email on her laptop."

"So, what are you waiting for? Go and arrest him. Why haven't you picked him up yet?"

Sara inclined her head. "The firm doesn't exist and we can't trace a Henry Barrows."

"Oh shit! How is that possible? How can someone deliberately set out to lure a young woman into a trap? What a sick individual... shit, I don't even want to go there. Why would he do this to Amber? She's a bit flighty at times, but basically, she's a nice enough girl. Why choose her?"

"Flighty? In what way?" Sara probed, trying to get to the depths of Amber's character.

"I don't know. She's what I would call eccentric, not your run-of-the-mill type of friend."

"That's not really telling me much."

She shrugged. "Sorry, that's all I can think of saying."

"It doesn't matter. Perhaps you can tell us where the interview was due to be held?"

"Nope. She said she had to catch a bus into town and someone would meet her outside a coffee house in the precinct. Honestly, I tried to tell her how suspicious that sounded, and no, this isn't me just saying it after the event. I truly tried to warn her about going to meet someone in such circumstances."

"And what was her reaction?"

"She outright told me that I was being jealous. That happened when we met up over the weekend. She'd forgiven me by the Monday and called me from the bus to say how excited, yet nervous, she felt. I knew better than to cast further doubts, so went along with the conversation, except I urged her to call me the second the interview ended. It was my way of trying to keep tabs on her. I spent the rest of the day being frantic until I received the call that afternoon, except it wasn't from her. My life fell apart. I was torn in two. But his voice and the sinister threat he issued will remain with me for the rest of my days. I apologise for not confiding in you sooner." Fresh tears cascaded. "Please, please, you have to help her. I know she's in danger. I don't know what this man is capable of, although I can imagine. She doesn't deserve this. No girl deserves to be abducted and kept against her will."

"Try not to imagine what she's possibly going through. Did you see the press appeal go out last night?"

"Yes. Again, I was filled with guilt and almost rang the number on the screen. To say what, I don't know. Actually, I do. I could've told you that I felt she'd been lured away. In truth, I thought you would come down heavy on me after how I reacted during our last meeting. I'm so confused right now. I want you to find Amber, but am I guilty of thinking of my own welfare before hers?"

"My take is that this person, or people, just wanted to keep you on your toes by threatening you. I could be wrong."

"I hope so, but you said you'd get me and my mum a safe place to stay. Is that still on the table?"

"Of course it is, I never go back on my word. Returning to the appeal, we received a couple of calls, one from a passenger on the bus who pointed us in your direction." Sasha frowned. "By that, I mean, he informed us that Amber was talking to someone, a friend on the phone and mentioned an interview. The other significant call we received was from a young lady who said she saw Amber walking through the precinct and then get in the back of a limousine."

Sasha gasped and covered her mouth, then dropped her hand. Her eyes wide with expectation, she asked, "There, that's something good for you to go on, isn't it? The number plate, you have that, don't you?"

"Sadly, nothing as detailed as that came from the witness. We're doing our very best to establish more information about the vehicle, don't worry."

"I'll keep thinking positive, then. God, what else can I do? I want her back home. I dread to think how she's being treated by this person. I doubt he's treating her kindly, not after abducting her. Am I wrong to think that?"

"Let's hope something puts us on the right track today. We're still receiving calls from the appeal, so all is not lost just yet. Right, I'm going to sort out some accommodation for you, give me five minutes." Sara excused herself and stepped into the hallway. She rang her contact at the station and was given the all-clear to use one of the safe houses situated on the outskirts of Hereford. Sara arranged for a member of the team to meet them at the location in a couple of hours. That would give Sasha and her mother time to pack a few essentials for a few days. Sara shared the news, and immediately, Sasha started panicking.

"God, I need to ring Mum. She's at work, her boss isn't going to be pleased."

"My advice would be for your mother to tell her boss she's facing a family emergency and can't go into detail right now."

"Good idea." Sasha picked up her mobile and pressed a single number. "Hi, Mum, sorry to trouble you at work, it's an emergency... No, you need to listen very carefully, I have the police here." Sasha rolled her eyes and held the phone away from her ear. "Mum, calm down. I haven't done anything wrong. I'll tell you what's happened when you get here... Yes, you need to come home straight away... Tell him it's a family emergency and you'll be back in a few days." Sasha held the phone away a second time when her mother started shouting again. "Mum, I'm not messing around, this is really serious... Okay, I'll see you soon... thank you for trusting me."

After she'd finished her call, she placed her mobile on the table. "I think I got through to her in the end. She's coming home, she should be here in about fifteen minutes. Do you want me to pack a bag while I'm waiting?"

"Why not? I'm sure your mother will understand once she learns the truth."

Sasha rose from the table. "I hope so. She can be a nightmare for weeks if she gets in a foul mood, and to be trapped in a strange house with her is going to do my head in."

"I'll have a word with her when she arrives, pave the way for you. How's that?"

"Thanks! I won't be long. Help yourself to tea or coffee, the milk's in the fridge and mugs are in the cupboard."

"We'll do that, do you want anything?"

"I've just had one, thanks." She smiled and left the room.

Sara busied herself making the drinks and turned to see Carla staring at the wall behind her. "Something wrong?"

Carla shook herself out of her daze. "Sorry, no, drifted off there for a moment. Did you say something?"

"I asked if you're okay." She switched the kettle on and returned to her seat.

"No. I'm fine. It wasn't personal, I swear. I was thinking about the case. Why would the abductor contact Sasha? Why take the risk? Why not leave well alone?"

Sara sighed as she thought. "Maybe his intention was to scare the crap out of her, keep her from immediately running to the police."

"Why?"

"To give him, or them, time to carry out their audacious plan, whatever that might be."

Carla puffed out her cheeks. "Sounds bloody ominous if that's the truth. What are we up against here?"

"I wish I knew." Sara lowered her voice and added, "Unless we figure out who that limo belongs to, I have a sinking feeling we'll never find out."

"God, don't say that. The thought of Amber being in this madman's hands..." Carla shuddered. "Shit! What if something like this had happened to me, you know, after I'd been attacked?"

"Try not to think about it, love. You're safe, injured but safe, that's the main thing."

"I wish I knew why and who carried out the assault. None of it makes sense to me."

"Nor me. I haven't forgotten about you, we will find out who did this and punish them, I assure you."

Carla waved a hand to dismiss the claim. "I'd rather leave it well alone, for fear it might stir up more trouble if we find out who's responsible."

"I get that, surely you want to see them punished?"

"Of course." Her gaze dropped to the table. "But after knowing what's happened to Amber, I'm just thankful I'm still around and able to do my job."

The kettle switched off, and Sara patted Carla's hand and leapt out of her chair to make the drinks.

The back door opened and a woman with long blonde hair entered and stopped dead. "Who are you and what are you doing in my kitchen?"

Sara produced her warrant card. "DI Sara Ramsey and my partner, DS Carla Jameson. We're waiting for Sasha..."

Before Sara had the chance to say anything else, her daughter entered the room. "Come on, Mum, upstairs, I'll explain everything while I help you pack a bag."

Sara smiled at Sasha, grateful to see she'd obviously had second thoughts about wanting Sara to pave the way for her.

"What?"

Sasha grabbed her mother's hand and pulled her out of the kitchen and up the stairs.

"She didn't seem too happy," Carla noted.

"She'll come around. She has to."

They finished their drinks and for the next ten minutes continued to bounce some ideas around about where the case might lead them, until they heard footfalls on the stairs.

Sara and Carla stood. The two women, carrying a holdall each, entered the room. "We're ready. Shall we take our car?" Sasha asked.

"Yes, that's probably a good idea."

They left the house and secured the back door. Sara and Carla jumped in Sara's car and Sasha and her mother followed them in theirs. Fifteen minutes later they arrived at the cottage, out near Creddenhill. A member of the witness protection team was already there, waiting for them.

Sara scanned the area, checking to see if they'd been followed to the location and then ushered everyone inside the cottage.

"It's cold, dark and horrible," Sasha's mother hissed through gritted teeth, obviously not warming to the idea they would need to stay here for the next few days, at least.

"Stop complaining, Mum, what's the alternative? Do you want what's happened to Amber to happen to me?"

"Don't be so absurd. Am I not allowed to voice my opinion now?"

Sasha hugged her mother. "I get that you're scared, I am as well, but we need to do as the officers say. That way, hopefully, we'll keep safe."

"I know. I'm sorry. I'm struggling to get my head around all of this. It's not right that people should be abducted, people I know. It's hard to take in, love, that's all."

"It's not ideal, none of this is, Mrs Minnow. We're doing our very best to keep both of you safe while we search for Amber. Hopefully, you'll only have to put up with the inconvenience for a few days, maximum."

"I hope so. Sorry for being such an idiot."

"There's no need for you to apologise. Do you two want to go with Carla and take your bags upstairs while I have a word with the officer?"

The three ladies left the room. Sara smiled at the tall officer. "Sorry, I should have introduced myself when we arrived. Sara Ramsey."

"No problem, I understood the need to get inside quickly. Drew Mitchell, at your service."

"Thanks, Drew. All this is new to me, I feel for Sasha and her mother. We've got this place for two days, is that right?"

"Yes, but give us a shout if you'd like to extend their stay."

"I will. Hopefully, that won't be necessary and we'll have caught the bastard by then."

"Any news on that front?"

"No. I've got my team working on the intricacies of the case. We put out an appeal in the media yesterday and received some important leads to sink our teeth into. Nothing has come of it so far, though."

"Well, good luck. Here's my card, I need to shoot off now. Tell the ladies to make themselves at home, use the heating as and when they need it. I put some essential food in the kitchen. There's a Co-op store in Bobblestock they can use to stock up, although my advice would be to keep their heads down for the next forty-eight hours and not to leave the cottage."

"I'll pass the message on. Thanks again for all your assistance."

Sara saw him to the front door and put the chain on after he left. She wandered into the galley kitchen with its exposed beams, matching those in the living room, and opened the fridge to see what supplies he'd left them. For a man, he'd chosen well. Carla joined her a few moments later. "How are they?"

"The upstairs is a bit tight, a few complaints from the mother about how dirty the bathroom was and that it wasn't up to her high standards. I left them to it."

"Typical of a house-proud mother, eh? It'll give her something to do during their stay."

They both laughed.

"This place is quite cute. Different to what's usually on offer, a flat in the centre of Hereford."

"It is. I wouldn't mind staying here for a few days myself, if the opportunity arises."

"Let's hope that doesn't happen," Carla said, shaking her head.

"Okay, I'll tell the ladies we're going to leave now. I'm eager to get back to the station, see if the team have uncovered anything new." She made her way back through the cottage again and shouted up the stairs. "Ladies, we're going to make a move. Is there anything you need before we go?"

Sasha appeared at the top of the steep stairs. "I don't think so. Umm… are there any rules we need to follow about living here?"

"Not really, I've got Drew's card, I'll leave it on the side-table by the inglenook. He's put a few essentials in the fridge, more than a few, actually, they'll see you through the next day or so. He also told me to tell you there's a Co-op at Bobblestock. My advice would be to limit the time you spend away from the cottage, just to be on the safe side. I'll leave you one of my cards as well, don't hesitate to ring me, all right?"

"Thank you, you're so kind. Are you going to try and find Amber now?"

"Of course. Oh, I almost forgot, Drew also said to tell you not to be afraid to use the heating. I felt the radiator, it's on, please be patient, it might take a little while to heat up an old house like this. Stay safe. I'll be in touch soon."

Sasha nodded and smiled. "I can't thank you enough for believing me."

Sara smiled. "We're in this together. See you later. Make sure you put the chain on the front door after we leave, just in case."

She collected Carla, and they left the cottage. Outside, she sucked in a lungful of crisp fresh air. "I hope they're going to be all right here."

"They should be, provided they follow the rules and remain tucked up inside."

Sara turned the radio on once they were back in the car. "It's almost time for the news, I'm hoping they'll still be running the appeal."

A couple of tracks later, the local news came on. Sara frowned when she heard the announcer say they had an update on the case they'd been following closely. Sara shot a quick glance at Carla and turned the radio up.

"We were contacted by a young lady who possibly witnessed Amber Rowse's abduction in the centre of Hereford on Monday. This is what mobile hairdresser, Davina Harding had to say..."

Sara listened to Davina give the same account she'd given her about Amber getting into the limousine and cringed. "Jesus, what is wrong with people? Why go to the damn press?"

"Come now, you know the bloody answer to that. Everyone wants their fifteen minutes of fame these days."

"Seriously? I would rather do without it. This isn't good, it could hamper our investigation now that she's mentioned the limo. Sod it, sod it, sod it." Sara bashed the steering wheel with the heel of her hand.

6

$\mathcal{H}$arvey was out on his own, a specific target in mind this time around. He parked his car outside the designated address and waited. As soon as the woman's vehicle showed up, he prepared to swoop. Gloves in place, he picked up the rope from the passenger seat and wrapped it around one hand. Then, he reached for the vial and needle. He worked rapidly to fill the needle with the clear liquid. All this was done within seconds of the woman's arrival. She exited the car and went to the boot. She retrieved a large bag and approached the front door of the house.

He made his move. Crouching behind the hedge outside the property until he stepped onto the path. "Hi, are you waiting for someone?"

The woman jumped, turned to smile and said, "Yes, I was told the owner of the house wanted a haircut. Do you know Henry?"

"I do. Here, I know where he keeps his spare key, I'll let you in." Harvey approached the woman; she seemed grateful for his assistance. He lifted up the front mat and showed her the key. "Told you." He stood and she inched back to allow him access to the front door.

Swiftly, he jabbed her in the neck and released the contents of the needle. Her legs instantly gave way beneath her. He caught her and slung her over his shoulder, grateful that the nights were drawing in early now. "That'll teach you to keep your mouth shut, bitch. Thought you'd stir up trouble for us, did you? Well, that didn't work out well in your favour, did it? Fame seekers are the pits."

He threw her onto the back seat of his car and jumped behind the steering wheel, his eyes darting around the area, making sure no one had seen him. Then, he drove out to the airfield at Leominster where his brother was waiting for him.

"You're an idiot, grabbing another one so soon," Daniel slated him.

"When I want your opinion, I'll ask for it. Now give me a hand."

Together, they bundled the woman's body into the plane. Harvey bound her hands and feet, and Daniel prepared the plane for take-off.

Harvey sat in the executive chair and poured himself a celebratory glass of whisky. He downed the contents in one gulp and leaned back against the headrest, satisfied his latest acquisition had gone so smoothly.

The plane landed, and together, they transferred the girl's unconscious body into the waiting vehicle and drove to the cottage.

"I'll check the other one is okay."

Daniel nodded, and Harvey left his brother arranging the girl in the chair in the kitchen.

Harvey opened the damp room and strained an ear in the dark. He detected a slight sniffle in the corner and switched on the light. Amber shielded her eyes from the sudden glare lighting up the room. "Hello, pretty lady. How are you?"

"Please, let me go. You've punished me enough now."

"Have I? How do you know that?"

"I want to go home."

"This is your home for the foreseeable future, until the next part of the plan slots into place. We have company for you."

"Who?"

He laughed. "Eager bunny, aren't you? You'll find out soon enough."

He left the room again, the door wide open, knowing that she was still chained to the bed and unable to escape.

Daniel was standing with his arms folded at the sink, staring at the girl. "She's pretty in an elf-like kind of way."

Harvey laughed. "How many pretty elves have you stumbled across in the past?"

"All right, smartarse. What now?"

"Help me get her in the same room as the other one."

"Is that wise?"

Harvey frowned. "Meaning?"

"What if they get talking and come up with a plan to escape?"

Harvey laughed. "Like that's going to happen. The bitch will be chained to the bed, like the other one. They ain't going anywhere soon. Not until we're ready to hand them over. Wait until I contact Shipman, he's gonna be rubbing his hands when I tell him we have two girls already. He might even bring the pick-up time forward a little, so we get our hands on the dosh earlier."

"That'll be good. The sooner the girls are off our hands, the better."

"You're such a wuss. I never hear you complaining when you're out there spending the bloody money we earn from doing this."

"It doesn't make it right."

"You're nuts. You want the spoils but baulk at the work involved achieving it."

"Bollocks. Sod off, bro."

"Make yourself useful. Knock up a meal for them."

"A meal? I ain't no chef."

Harvey sighed. "You want me to do all the work, is that it?"

"Hardly, I fly the damn plane, don't I? You can't do that because you didn't have the guts to take the lessons."

"We both have our uses then. Just do it. There should be a can of tomato soup in the cupboard, that'll do for them. I think there's some stale bread next to it, they can dunk it in the soup."

Daniel pointed at the girl in the chair. "How long before she wakes up?"

"I'll get her settled and inject her with the reverse serum. Get on with the food. I want to be back in Hereford within a few hours."

Harvey hauled the girl over his shoulder and wound his way

through the small cottage to the cave room at the rear. "Here, I've brought some company for you. Budge over, you're going to have to share the bed."

Amber squeezed into the corner and studied the girl.

Harvey grabbed the piece of chain he had hidden earlier from under the bed and attached it to the girl's right leg. Then, he injected her with the serum and stood back. Her head slowly rotated, and she jumped when she saw Amber.

"Who are you? Oh, God, you're that girl I saw getting in…" she whispered. "Where am I?"

"You're safe, that's all you need to know," Harvey informed her. "Dinner will be here soon."

"Thank you," Amber muttered from the corner. She held her hand out to the other girl. "My name is Amber."

"Thank God you're alive."

"I am."

Davina glanced Harvey's way and asked, "Why are you doing this to us?"

He pointed at her. "You shouldn't have opened your mouth to the press."

"Oh no! You're punishing me because I helped the police?"

"Yep." He left the room and returned to the kitchen. Daniel was in the process of tipping the soup into a couple of cereal bowls. Harvey selected a few slices of the stale loaf, picked off a couple of mouldy bits and threw the bread into the soup. "There, a meal fit for a princess or two."

7

---

*F*riday morning arrived, and so did the torrential rain. Sara hated the rain, it soured everyone's mood. Today, she decided to look on the bright side; at least she wasn't driving into work battling a snow blizzard like the people in America. She'd heard the reports on the news and knew they'd be expecting the same weather front in the next ten days or so, if history was about to repeat itself.

The team were already at their desks and Carla appeared to be a lot brighter than the previous day. "Morning all, anything useful come in overnight?"

"No, nothing as yet," Carla replied. She left her seat and walked over to the vending machine to buy Sara a coffee.

"Thanks, Carla, nice to see I have you well-trained. You're looking so much better today, or is that the result of another bout of heavy make-up?"

"No, it's the Arnica gel I've been slathering on when I get home. Miracle stuff."

"I'll add it to my shopping list." Sara smiled and took a sip of her drink. "Where did we get up to with the limo yesterday?"

Will waved a sheet of paper. "I'm going through the list right now. There are fifty potentials to sift through."

"It's too much to ask that one of them belongs to Henry Barrows, am I right?"

Will shook his head as he cast his eyes over the list again. "Yep. Nothing on here."

"Just as I thought. In that case, Craig, we're relying on you to come up with the goods as usual."

"No pressure there, then. I didn't receive the footage until late afternoon. I'll get on it now and give you a shout as soon as I find anything."

"I'll leave you to it and continue with my daily grind. Once I've dealt with the post, we'll have a conflab about what we should do next. To say I was disappointed with the response from the public would be a gross understatement." She left her colleagues to it and drifted into her office, pausing for a few seconds to admire the view of the Brecon Beacons and their inviting peaks. She took a couple of sips of coffee and then sat behind her desk, sighing at the pile of brown envelopes vying for her attention.

Carla came into the room to rescue her from the mundane chore a little while later. "I've just received a call that you'll want to hear about."

Sara frowned. "Go on."

"I've had a Diane Watson on the phone."

"Who's she? Stop stringing it out longer than necessary, Carla."

"It's in connection with the appeal, well, sort of."

Sara opened her upturned hands. "And?"

"And… she got our number from her friend's room."

"Carla, can we hurry this up please?"

Carla swallowed. "Her friend, or should I say, flatmate, is Davina Harding."

"Now, you've grabbed my attention. What about her?"

"She's gone missing. Didn't come home last night."

Sara shot out of her chair and paced in front of her desk. "I knew it was wrong of her to go before the damn cameras. Bloody idiot. Sorry, I shouldn't say that, not when the young woman has gone missing, but bloody hell, this sort of thing boils my piss. Why do people persist in putting themselves in danger like this?"

"Would there be any point in me telling you to calm down?"

Sara closed her eyes and inhaled and exhaled a few deep breaths. "Sorry, I shouldn't let it affect me personally, but sometimes, people infuriate me."

"I can tell." Carla chuckled. "I told Diane we'd pop round to see her."

Sara tore her coat off the rack and marched past Carla into the incident room. Carla trotted behind her and grabbed her jacket off the back of her chair.

"We'll be back soon, hopefully," Sara shouted over her shoulder. She was in that much of a rush she bumped into DCI Carol Price at the top of the stairs.

"Whoa, slow down. What's going on?"

"Sorry, Ma'am, we've got another possible abduction. We're just on our way out to interview the woman's flatmate now."

"Another one. Any news on the first girl?"

"Yes and no. Sorry, I really need to go, can I drop by and fill you in later?"

"Yes, okay. Make sure you do. I take it the public hasn't proved to be much help with this investigation?"

"Again, let me share the details with you when we get back, if that's okay?"

"Suits me. Good luck."

"Thanks." Sara flew down the stairs at breakneck speed.

*T*hey arrived at Diane Watson's flat in record time. The young woman was obviously watching out for them and opened the door before Sara had the chance to knock.

"I'm so glad you're here and taking this seriously. At first, I had my doubts about calling you, but I started driving myself crazy and figured it would be better to ring you. Oh God, I'm going on, my mother is always telling me to take frequent breaths, but I can't help it.

Come in, do you want a drink? I've had to have a brandy to try and calm my nerves."

"No, it's a little early in the day for us, thanks for the offer, though. Can we sit down somewhere?"

"Oh my, I'm sorry. Yes, come into the lounge."

She showed them into a room decorated with a lot of what could only be described as fairy lights. Sara wondered if they had been put up at Christmas and forgotten about. "Why don't you tell us what you know and we'll go from there?"

"I stayed at my boyfriend's last night, well, I was supposed to. We had a row and I returned home early. I was disappointed not to see Davina here when I got back. Shrugged it off, thinking that she was possibly out with her brother. I must have fallen asleep on the sofa, it's been a hectic couple of weeks at work, so it was to be expected, then the falling out with Dan, well, it sapped all the energy out of me."

"I see. When did you realise Davina was missing?"

"This morning. I checked her room, her bed hadn't been slept in. She always tells me when she's going to see her brother, but she hadn't mentioned it."

"Does she have a boyfriend?"

"No. She's in between fellas, got stung badly by the last one, so she's been a little wary of them for a while."

"And you've tried contacting her?"

"Yes, I rang her mobile, but it keeps going into voicemail. She never turns the damn thing off, another reason for me to be concerned. It's just that, what with this other girl going missing and her speaking out in the press about it, I warned her not to. She thought it would be free advertising for her business."

Sara frowned. "Her business?"

"Yes, she's a mobile hairdresser, hence why she never switches off her phone. She gets dozens of calls, maybe a slight exaggeration there, in the evening. When you're self-employed, you don't get a minute to yourself, do you?"

"I can imagine. When was the last time you had any contact with her?"

"Yesterday afternoon. I rang her at about three, asked her if her tactics had worked and she was over the moon with the result. Said she had a few appointments that she needed to chase up that afternoon. She was grateful for the extra work the stint on TV had brought in as business had been drying up lately."

"Did she tell you where the new appointments were?"

"No, she didn't go into detail. Please, I have a bad feeling about this. She's usually uber-reliable and to have her disappear like this, it's got me thinking, and not in a good way."

Sara smiled, doing her best to put the young woman at ease. "Don't worry, we have a few more questions we need to ask before we get the ball rolling."

Diane chewed on a nail. "What sort of questions? I've told you everything I know. You need to get out there and try to find her. If this person has kidnapped her... oh God, I dread to think what he's going to do to her. Have you found the other girl yet?"

"No, we're still trying to trace her. Maybe you can tell me a little about her ex-boyfriend?"

"What can I tell you? He was a wanker with a capital W. I hated him, and the way he treated her was bloody appalling. Didn't have a decent bone in his body from what I could tell, but Davina was smitten with him. Couldn't see anything wrong in him until she found him in bed with one of her so-called friends. I could see it coming. He made my skin crawl, the way he kept eyeing me up when he came around here. She couldn't see any wrong in him, no matter what I said."

"Does he have a name?"

"Steve Abbot, he lives a stone's throw from here at Dawson Road, number four, I think it is, you might want to check on that."

Carla scribbled down the information in her notebook.

"When was the last time Davina had any form of contact with him?"

"Back in November, it was his birthday. She foolishly took a present around to him."

"Is she in the habit of giving her exes presents after breaking up with them?"

"No, she'd already bought it for him and rather than see it go to waste, she dropped it off."

"And how was her visit received?"

"He rejected her at the front door. She came home here in tears, threw the present in the bin and swore herself off men for life."

"He sounds a heartless sort. Any form of contact between them since? A phone call, chance meeting perhaps?"

"No, nothing that she's admitted to. I think she was well shot of him and realised that she'd be better off without him in her life after he refused her present. She was upset for a few weeks, but I gave her a good talking to, told her to stop dwelling on the past and look forward. Someone nice will come along, sooner or later, they always do, right?"

Sara nodded, recalling how her husband Mark had drifted into her life when she had been least expecting it. "How likely do you think her disappearance has anything to do with the ex?"

"I don't know, one minute I think he's behind it and then I find myself disputing it the next. I wanted to tell you about it, so you have the information to hand to deal with it as how you see fit."

"Excellent, we'll definitely delve into it. And what did her brother have to say?"

"About Steve?"

"Sorry, no, I meant about her going missing. But okay, what was his perception about her ending things with Steve?"

"He was eager for them to break up, he hated the bloke for the way he treated Davina. I rang him this morning, he said she hasn't contacted him for a few days, presumed she was busy. He saw her on the news and was dubious as to whether she'd done the right thing or not as well. He's mortified she's gone missing. Said he was going to get out there to search the streets for her."

"Therefore, there wouldn't be any point in us showing up at his house to question him. Do you have his phone number?"

Diane left her seat and picked up her mobile from the small coffee table. "Let me see. Here you are, Patrick Harding." She angled the phone for Carla to take down the number.

Carla nodded. "Thanks, I've got it."

"We'll reach out to him once we've left here. I take it they're close to each other."

"Yes, their parents are sadly no longer with us. They died from different forms of cancer a couple of years ago. Davina and her brother have been inseparable ever since. Maybe that was the wrong word to use, it's not like they live in each other's pocket, but yes, they're extremely close."

"Close enough that Patrick might go round to see Steve, blame him for her disappearance?"

She gasped. "Shit! I never thought about that. Please, you need to get round there, just in case. I'd hate for Patrick to get into trouble because of that scumbag."

"I hear you. Is there anything else you can tell us?"

"You might want to put out an alert on Davina's car, or is that me trying to tell you how to conduct an investigation?"

Sara smiled. "No, that would be one of the first things we look into, but thanks for the tip. What's the make, model and reg number?"

"Shit, I knew you were going to ask me that. I've got a recent photo of it on my phone, she's only had it a few months." She scrolled through her photos and showed Sara.

"It's a silver Ford Ka. I've got a partial plate, Carla. TG46. That's brilliant, it's a start anyway." Sara stood and Carla followed.

Diane led the way to the front door and opened it with a sigh. "I hope you find her, and soon. Will you let me know?"

"Of course. Thanks for calling us in the first place. Try not to worry too much."

"Yeah, right. I'll be going out of my mind until I get the call to say she's safe. Good luck."

Sara waved and marched back to the car. "We need to issue an alert for her vehicle ASAP."

"I'll ring Jill now."

"You do that and I'll call the brother, see if I can get hold of him." As it wasn't raining, Sara chose to make her call outside the car. "Hello, would that be Patrick Harding?"

"It is. Who is this? If you've got my sis—"

99

"Sir, I'm DI Sara Ramsey. It's about your sister. I've just left her flatmate, Diane. She informed me that you're out there, searching for your sister now."

"That's right. I had no intention of hanging around, waiting for the police to show up."

"I'm sorry you feel you don't have faith in our abilities, sir."

"I didn't say that. I'm entitled to be out here, you can't stop me."

"You're right, I can't stop you, but what I can do is ask you to rein in your emotions and think about this carefully."

"What are you saying?"

"That you need to work with us and not jump in feet first. What would you do if you discovered your sister?"

"I'd take her home with me."

"And supposing the person who is holding your sister, if that's the case, has a weapon and puts up a fight to keep her?"

"I did boxing in my youth, I know how to handle myself, Inspector."

"I don't doubt that, sir, but it's not the way to go. Let's meet up and decide between us what the next course of action should be."

"You do your shit and I'll do mine. She's all I have now our parents are gone. I'm not about to let a crazed lunatic do unimaginable things to her, not if I can help it."

"That's gallant behaviour, I can't dispute it, but it's the wrong way to handle the situation."

"In your opinion… you forgot to add that part."

"Patrick, I'm pleading with you, don't do this alone."

The phone went dead. "Shit, damn and blast. I handled that well, not." Sara opened the car door and slumped into her seat, defeated.

"Jill has got the car details and is in the process of circulating the information now."

"I'm glad something is going to plan. I screwed up with the brother. He hung up on me."

"Did he say where he was?"

"No, out and about, scouring Hereford. I'm presuming he's searching the city centre and the surrounding area."

Carla wrinkled her nose. "It can't be helped, Sara, there's no point beating yourself up. Put yourself in his shoes. I recall you did exactly the same when Mark went missing a few years ago."

"Not exactly, but yes, okay, I'll give you that one. The key to this is to find that damn car. Maybe the kidnapper lured her to meet him somewhere under false pretences. Sasha highlighted the same, if I recall rightly."

"Possibly. We need to check Davina's phone records, see what shows up."

Sara shot out of the car again and ran back to the flat. She hammered on the front door, and a startled Diane answered it. "Have you found her?"

"No, sorry to get your hopes up unnecessarily. I need Davina's phone number so we can trace her calls."

"Of course, I don't know it off the top of my head, let me get my phone."

Sara stepped inside the house and withdrew her notebook from her pocket. Diane reappeared and called out Davina's number.

"I hope it helps."

Sara smiled. "I'm sure it will. I'll be in touch soon. By the way, I've just rung her brother, he hung up on me. I get the impression he doesn't have much faith in the police."

"I'm not sure. He's a very emotional man. Losing his parents rocked his world, and Davina's come to that."

"Okay, thanks for this, Diane." She ran back to the car, started the engine and headed back towards the station. On the way, Carla rang ahead and instructed the team to get working on tracing the calls made to Davina's phone and finding the young woman's car on the ANPR system from the day before.

*I*t was a couple of hours before Sara was informed that a patrol car had located Davina's vehicle in a quiet cul-de-sac on the other side of town. "Get SOCO over there ASAP, Carla. We need to conduct a house-to-house in the road as well, someone must have seen something. I go back to my first thought, that maybe the kidnapper lured her to that location with the intention of abducting her. Barry and Marissa, will you handle that?"

"Of course. Shall we go now?" Barry asked.

"Yep. Let's keep on top of things as they happen, what with time being of the essence and all that."

The two officers slipped on their jackets and headed off.

"Craig, anything at all about this limo yet?"

"I've managed to trace it on CCTV. I'm in the process of following the route it took."

"Excellent news. Any sign of a clear registration number or is that wishful thinking on my part?"

"I caught a glimpse of a part of it, ran it through the system, but nothing came back. Either I wrote it down wrongly or they used a false plate. My instinct is telling me it's the latter, but I'll keep trying. I'm nearly there, boss."

"Okay, let me know as soon as you can. Anyone got anything else for me?"

The rest of the team either shook their heads or shrugged. *Damn, either this git has a well-thought-out plan, or he's a professional.* "Jill, can you check the database, see if there are any similar cases we should be looking into in this area, say over the past five years?"

"Sorry to disappoint you, boss, I already did that and drew a blank."

"Great. What the heck is going on and who is behind these bloody crimes?" Sara swept a hand through her hair and tugged a few strands in annoyance.

"There's no point getting yourself worked up," Carla whispered. "It's not going to help."

"It'll make me feel better, punishing myself for not cracking this damn case by now. Two young women go missing, one because she probably opened her goddamn mouth to the press, and we're no further forward. Help me out, guys, where do we go from here if we can't trace that limo? It's the only real clue we have that could possibly lead us to the perpetrator."

The team all stared at her. That was the frustrating part, the lack of clues or leads for them to tackle.

"We need to start dissecting things, see if that helps. All we have to hand is Amber's computer, her phone records, and we're in the process of getting Davina's records as well. At least, we've located the second victim's vehicle. Maybe Barry and Marissa will have a bit of luck when they chat to the people living in that area," Carla summarised.

"And if they don't? We're up the creek, paddleless. I'm going to run it past the chief. I'm fearful of losing momentum on this one. I think we should work over the weekend, if you're all up for it. What say you?"

"I'm up for it. Maybe run a skeleton staff, some of us might already have plans for the weekend," Carla was quick to suggest.

"Any volunteers?" Sara asked, hopeful that at least some of them would agree, should the chief give the go-ahead on using up a quota of their overtime during these tough financial times.

Craig never let her down, he was the first to raise his hand. "I don't mind, boss. It's the dead of winter, after all. I might not have been so forthcoming if there was the prospect of having a heatwave at the weekend."

Sara laughed. "Thanks, Craig. Anyone else?"

"I'll do it," Carla offered, eventually.

"No, you should get some rest."

"Bollocks. I need to be here, trying to track this bastard down."

Sara raised her hands; on the one hand, she was delighted with her partner's response, and on the other, she couldn't help worrying that Carla was pushing herself too hard, willing to remain at work rather than be at home, due to the bashing she'd received a few days before. A place which should be deemed as safe and secure to a copper. "All right, I'm not going to argue with you. Let me get the all-clear from the chief and we'll go from there." From her own perspective, she hoped Mark wasn't going to kick up a stink when she broke the news. There was no reason to think that way, he'd always been very easy-going with her working overtime in the past, before they'd tied the knot, but she was wary about pushing the boundaries all the same. Happy husband, happy life!

She paid the chief a visit. Recapped the two investigations she was running and her frustrations at hoping to get the girls back swiftly, along with implementing the necessity for some of her team to work over the weekend, to keep on top of the cases. The chief didn't seem too happy with the request but, in the end, she reluctantly agreed it was the right course of action, if there was any hope of finding the two girls alive.

Sara relayed the news to her team and accepted Craig and Carla's suggestion that they should join her. Now, all she had to do was break the news to Mark. She decided the best way for her to do that was over a nice steak dinner and a glass of wine. She rang him at work. "Sorry to disturb you."

"It's fine. I was just thinking about you. Thought we'd go out somewhere nice over the weekend."

"Hmm... about that, going out, I mean. Sorry, love, I was going to break the news to you gently over dinner tonight, but I have to work this weekend."

Silence greeted her for a few seconds until Mark let out a long sigh. "If you must, I was looking forward to spending some quality time with you. Do you really have to give up your entire weekend?"

"I'll have to see how it goes. The sooner we catch this bastard, the safer the women of Hereford are going to be, in my mind at least."

"I get that. Ignore me, I'm just being selfish. No doubt I can find something to do around here to keep me occupied. Or I could pay your parents a visit, see if they need any urgent chores doing. I know your father's been ill this week."

"You're a good man, Mark. I was full of trepidation about breaking the news to you."

"Why? I'm not a tyrant, Sara. I've never had a pop at you about your work before, have I?"

"I know and I appreciate it. I still want to cook you a nice meal this evening, to make up for letting you down."

"Correction, you've done no such thing. I won't try to dissuade you from cooking, though."

"How about I stop off at the supermarket on the way home and grab us a couple of nice steaks?"

"Sounds good to me. I have a late appointment this evening, I should be home at around seven."

"Excellent, gives me enough time to shop and make a start on the meal. I've gotta run now. Thanks for understanding, Mark, I knew there was a reason why I married you."

"Get away with you. Marriage is about compromising, isn't it? I foresee us having to do a lot of that over the years to come, given our demanding careers."

"We'll do our best not to let that happen though, yes?"

"You have my word. See you later. Love you."

"Love you, too."

She hung up and immediately dialled her mother's number to ask how her father was doing. "Sorry, Mum, I was hoping to drop in and see you both over the weekend, but I need to work."

"That's all right, dear, needs must, eh? No news on that missing girl, I take it?"

"Not yet, no. Mark's going to be at a loose end, he's planning on popping around to see if you have any chores for him to do."

"If he's sure. The jobs are mounting up around here, since your father became ill."

"Just make a list. Sorry I won't get a chance to pop in and see you. Looking forward to next weekend though, Mum."

"I know you do your best, love. Take care. Speak soon."

Sara ended the call with a smile on her face and an ache in her heart, knowing that she wouldn't be able to check on her father's health in person over the weekend.

8

---

*H*arvey clapped his hands and then fisted the air in triumph. "I finally did it."

Daniel stared at him, trying to figure out what he was on about. "Spill, the suspense is killing me."

"That bird from the solicitor's up the road."

Daniel shrugged. "What about her?"

Harvey exhaled noisily. "She's finally agreed to come on a date with me."

"Oh, right. Don't tell me, she's your next victim."

Harvey frowned. "Why the pissed off tone? What if she is? Have you got something to say about that?"

"Nope, forget I said anything. I'll be glad when all this is over. Hate being on tenterhooks all the time, wondering if the coppers are going to track us down."

"Why should they? Up to now we've been super cautious. They're busy chasing their tails, I've got no intention of giving them anything useful to latch on to in their hunt for us, either. You need to learn to relax, bro, and leave all the nitty-gritty to me. Have I ever let you down before?"

Daniel sighed and hitched up a shoulder. "I suppose. I need to get my own life on track, Harvey."

"What are you saying? You want to pull out?"

"Maybe." Daniel threw a pen across his desk. "I don't know. I don't like the idea of those two girls being alone in that house, with barely any food or water. It's not right. What if something happens to them?"

"Such as what? They're chained to the frigging bed, numpty." Harvey prodded his temple as if insinuating Daniel was thick.

"About that, you think it's right to treat them worse than we'd treat an animal?" Daniel shouted.

"Are you for real? Who cares how the frigging girls are treated? I don't. As long as we get the money that's owed us in the end, that's what's keeping me going. The thought of all that lovely dosh running through my fingers. Money, the root of all evil." He let out a sinister laugh.

"The sign of evil, Mum always says. I'm still not au fait with this, bro. Can't we bring the hand-over day forward? Why do we have to keep the girls, feed them et cetera for longer than a week? It doesn't make sense, none of this does."

"And that, dear bro, is why I'm the perceived brains of this outfit and not you." He leapt out of his chair and jabbed his finger in Daniel's chest. "I'm in charge. I'm the one with the contacts and the nous to pull this off. Left up to you, that plane wouldn't leave the airfield."

"About that. We need juice and I don't have the funds to fill her up."

"Take it out of petty cash." He returned to his chair and dug around in the drawer next to him, threw the tin at his brother and sniggered.

"You're such a fucking moron at times. It was a genuine dilemma, one that I'd like an answer to; instead, you bloody insult my intelligence, not for the first time. It's becoming problematic, Harvey."

"Oo... big words for you. I'll transfer some funds from my bank account to the business account, which is lacking at present."

"And where did you get that kind of money? You're always pleading poverty."

"Shipman may have bunged me an upfront payment."

Daniel sat upright in his chair. "What? And you didn't think to mention it? What am I? Your lackey or your damn business partner?"

"Not five minutes ago, you were telling me you wanted out, so you bloody need to make your mind up. I've had it with your whining, Daniel. If you want out, then I can arrange that, no problem, but don't come running to me when your bank balance runs dry."

Daniel picked up another pen and tapped it on his legal-sized notepad. "You think you've got one over on me, you're wrong, bro. I'm going to bide my time and leave you at your most vulnerable."

Harvey laughed and shook his head. "See, even divulging that tells me how fucking naïve you are."

"Screw you."

"I've tried, I don't tend to get as much satisfaction doing it that way." He tipped his head back and laughed like a crazed hyena.

Daniel shook his head. "You're sick."

"Careful, you keep saying that and I'm likely to take offence."

"Fuck off."

"Okay. I'll leave you to finish up here, I have a date to prepare for."

"Warped shit! Date my arse."

"A date with destiny." He tucked his chair under the desk, slipped on his jacket and headed out of the door.

He waved at his open-mouthed brother through the window and jumped in his car. Driving home, he put on some Ed Sheeran to get him in the mood for what lay ahead of him. However, he found himself distracted, recapping the conversation he'd had with his twin. He needed Daniel, if only for the use of his plane. How could he likely circumvent not using him? He wracked his brain and failed to think of a different option.

Once he was at home, he showered, dressed in a grey pin-striped suit and ran through how he predicted the evening ahead might pan out. *Shit! I should've checked if Daniel would be available for later on, knowing what a foul mood he was in when I left.*

He punched his brother's number into his mobile. "Hi, yeah, just checking if you'll be free later."

"Oh, right, so I do have my uses after all."

"Don't be so pathetic, Daniel. I need to know that you won't let me down."

"Have I ever let you down before? Think carefully, bro."

"No, never. Does that mean you're not going to start?"

"Yep, I've got your back as always, for now. I'll fill the plane up and be ready from nine o'clock onwards. Text me when you can to let me know when to expect you."

"You're the best, Daniel. All this will be worth your while, I promise."

"It'd better be."

Harvey ended the call and did a little jig on the spot. Having his brother on board would help the evening be the success he projected it to be. He dabbed aftershave on his freshly shaven chin and stood back to admire what was on offer. "She's gonna be thrilled with the results, big man. You've got this."

He left his home and drove the short distance to where he'd arranged to meet the luscious Layla. He had volunteered to pick her up from her house, but she'd insisted that wasn't necessary and that she'd prefer to meet at a public location. He'd played along, telling her that she was doing the right thing in the current climate.

His driver dropped him across the street from the Miller and Carter restaurant and Layla appeared as he approached the restaurant. He leaned forward and kissed her cheek, which instantly warmed beneath his lips. "You look incredible. I'm not late, am I?"

"Thank you. If you're late then so am I. Shall we go in? It's freezing out here."

She wasn't dressed for a winter evening. She wore a slinky knee-length black glitter dress, accessorised with a silver shawl wrapped around her shoulders. Very smart and sexy as hell. His erection sprang to attention, his excitement mounting at what would come later.

"Come, let's get you inside before you freeze to death. I appreciate the effort you put in for my benefit."

"Oh, no, I always dress up when I go out for a meal. It's the way I was brought up by my parents. Can't stand people, men in particular, who casually show up in ripped jeans and expect their dates to be okay with their appearance."

"I'm the same. Jeans are for a date at the bowling alley, do you bowl?"

"I've been known to, in the past, not that I'm any good. Thank you for making the effort, I would've felt awkward had you not worn a suit this evening."

"The pleasure is all mine. I hope we make a connection this evening, I've been dying to ask you out for months." He opened the front door and gestured for her to go ahead of him.

She giggled. "I know you have. My mum always tells me to 'treat men mean to keep them keen'."

"And how is that advice working out?"

She waved her hand from side to side. "Unsuccessfully, so far."

The host welcomed them. "Do you have a table booked?"

"Yes, I booked it earlier today in the name of Davis," Layla replied.

"Ah, yes, I have it here. If you'd care to follow me."

Harvey glanced around at the early diners tucking into their sumptuous meals. The smiles on their faces told him he was in for a treat, in more ways than one this evening. He held Layla's chair out for her, charmer that he was.

The waiter appeared at their table to take their drink orders. "What would you like? Shall I get a bottle of prosecco?" Harvey asked.

Layla smiled her approval. "Sounds delightful."

After the waiter had left, she leaned forward and whispered, "We're sharing the bill. I need you to understand that I'm an independent woman of means."

He snorted. "Oh, is that so? We'll decide later."

She shook her head and narrowed her eyes. "Either we agree the point now or I walk out of here."

He was taken aback by the harshness of her tone. He hated bossy women, punishing her was going to be his absolute pleasure. He turned on the charm and grinned. "If you insist, I know when I'm beaten."

"I do. And, thank you. Now, the taxing question is, what do we choose from their excellent menu?"

"My preference has always been to plump for their finest steak. How does that sound to you?"

Her finger ran down the menu and paused at the dish he'd suggested. She tapped it a few times and then trailed her finger back across the other dishes on offer. "I'm not sure I'm in the mood for a steak tonight. I'm not really one for consuming a lot of red meat. I think I'll have the chicken fillet instead."

He glanced at the menu and noted the price; the dish she'd chosen was one of the cheapest available. "Looks tempting, I must say. No, I'm a man of my word, I tend to stick with my initial option when there's a choice to be made."

"Admirable quality," she replied, "I fear I'm a bit of a ditherer, especially where choosing a meal is concerned."

"What about your everyday life? You seem a very astute lady to me."

She smiled as the waiter reappeared to take their orders. Harvey requested the meals they'd selected, and the man drifted off again. "Sorry, you were saying?"

"I suppose I have a certain skill for detecting what's wrong in a person, at least, I've been known to in the past."

"I see. Are you saying you've never made a mistake when deciding if a male companion has the makings of a good boyfriend or not?"

She sat back and laughed. "I wouldn't go as far as to say that. Tell me about yourself, I've known you a few months now, since you and your partner opened up the office down the road from where I work, how's it going there?"

"I can't complain, and my partner is my twin brother. Although to look at us, you wouldn't believe it."

"Wow, I would never have guessed if you hadn't told me. So you're not identical twins. Who's the oldest, you or him?"

"Me. Which gives me the right to boss him around."

They both laughed. He admired her gleaming white teeth and the cute dimple that appeared in her flushed cheeks.

"What sort of work do you do?"

"We're financial experts. There's not a lot we don't know about stocks and shares and a few secret money-making ventures that I can't discuss."

"Oh, why's that?"

"If I divulged any secrets, then I'd be forced to kill you," he told her with a straight face. Her horrified expression made him chuckle. "Sorry, my idea of a joke. Please forgive me. Upon reflection it was probably something I shouldn't have mentioned on a first date."

"Or any date," she chastised. Her smile had disappeared and was replaced by a scowl.

He soon realised he'd overstepped the mark and dug deep for a charm offensive. "So, tell me what you like to do in your spare time."

She toyed with the stem of her wine glass for a moment or two before responding, "I like to keep fit. I've seen you and your brother down at the gym, that's where I first noticed you."

"You have?" He cast his mind back, trying to recollect seeing her there. He couldn't, but he lied and said, "Ah, yes, I knew I recognised you from somewhere other than the solicitor's. Do you go there often? I'm guessing with a stunning figure like that, at least a couple of times a week, am I right?"

She sniggered. "Yes, I try to get down there at least three nights a week, depending on my work schedule. Sometimes my boss asks me to remain behind and type up an urgent report he needs for court the following day. I never like to refuse."

"Why? You're entitled to have a life of your own outside office hours, aren't you?"

"You're right, of course. It's just that if I said no, I know he'd take offence and do all that he could to get rid of me."

"What makes you say that? It hardly seems fair to me."

"I'm assuming it would be the case because he sacked my predecessor for doing the same thing. She put a family dinner before working overtime for Christopher and she was fired the next morning."

"Jesus, what a tyrant of a boss. Not sure I could work for anyone that rigid. You need to have a good rapport with your staff to get the best out of them."

"I think you're right. I tend to keep my head down at work, do what I'm told when I'm told and no backchat. I detest it sometimes. Wish I could find another role more suited for my skills, but jobs are hard to come by since the lockdown last year. The economy is still in a bad way."

"Hey, you don't have to tell me that. I'm a financial expert, remember? My brother and I are always on the lookout for skilled workers. I think you'd be the perfect fit. We need a bossy boots to keep us in order." He laughed. "You want to see the state of our filing system, correction, we don't have one and we're in dire need of one that works."

Layla tutted. "Sounds like there's a real mess to sort out. I'm not sure I would be the right person to tackle that for you. Anyway, I really do love my work at the solicitor's. I get to read all the court documents as I type them, real eye-openers some of them, I can tell you."

"Oh, do tell."

The waiter arrived, interrupting their conversation again. He deposited their steak and chicken, asked if they'd like any accompaniments and then departed when they gave their answers.

"Go on, I'm eager to hear," Harvey prompted.

She shook her head and stabbed her fork into a skinny chip. "I can't, I'm sworn to secrecy."

"That's a pity. Maybe your tongue will loosen after a few glasses of wine."

Another shocked expression. "No, definitely not."

She tucked into her meal, using extra force to cut the chicken into pieces than he thought was probably necessary. *She's a feisty one. One wrong word and she takes umbrage. I'm going to have to watch what I say and do. I need to keep her onside for later.*

"Tell me about your parents, are they still with us?"

"Of course they are, how old do you think I am?" she snapped.

He placed a hand on his chest, pretending to be mortified. "I'm sorry, the words slipped out. It's just that my parents died when I was a mere teenager." He lied, working on her sympathy gene to get him out of a hole.

He succeeded.

She slid a hand over his. "I'm sorry. I can be such a bitch at times. I didn't mean to snap at you, please forgive me?"

He pulled her hand up to his mouth and kissed the back of it. "Nothing to forgive. This is some first date, isn't it? I keep raising subjects that entice you to bite my head off. Maybe we should call it a night instead."

"Oh, no. Please, don't do that. Believe it or not, I'm really enjoying myself. I know I need to control my emotions. My dad is always telling me the same."

"Oh, okay, I thought you weren't having fun. Why don't we start over again, put all this behind us? Stick to safer subjects to discuss, like the weather perhaps?" He laughed, and she joined in.

"You call that a safe subject. I could talk for England on that topic."

"There, problem solved then. You first, which season do you prefer?"

"It has to be autumn, the beautiful changing of the leaves, marking the dormant season which lies ahead. I have this picture on my bedroom wall. It was a photo my grandfather took many years ago whilst on a trip to the States. He stopped off at a lake and the reflection is, well, simply magical. The different rust-coloured trees reflected in the still water, it was difficult to see where the tree line ended, if you get my drift?"

"What a wonderful experience. I'd love to travel around America, but I wouldn't know where to begin. We visited the usual tourist attractions when we were kids, such as Disney World, not that I can remember much, apart from the size of the meals and the number of restaurants there were around at the time."

"Was that before you lost your parents?"

"Yes, that's right. They died a few years later. Sorry…" He wiped away a fake tear that was intended to gain an extra dose of sympathy.

"It's okay. Have you spoken to anyone about your grief?"

"I've tried over the years, but when it came to the crunch, I didn't have it in me to attend the sessions."

"That's so sad. I wish I could help alleviate your pain and grief."

He smiled, relieved he'd managed to hook her interest again. "I have good days and bad. I have my brother to ease me through the bouts of grief. He's more emotional than me about our loss, so I've always had to remain strong for his sake. Sometimes, it's good to be alone and just let the sorrow pour out of me."

"Any time you want to release your pent-up feelings, I'm always here for you. Everyone needs a way of venting their emotions, it's not good to bottle them up."

"You're very kind. Most of the time, I'm fine. Let's change the subject again, I don't want to be maudlin on our first date, this should be a time to rejoice. Tell me, do you like to visit the theatre?"

"Oh yes, I love it. My good friend and I sometimes book a weekend away in London. We get a thrill from visiting the sites and taking in a musical in the evening."

"Ah, I'm not really one for musicals. I do, however, love a good Agatha Christie show; my brother and I venture up to London now and again, too. Maybe next time we go, we could go as a group. Is your friend single?"

"Cherry would die if I set her up on a blind date weekend."

"Oh, I didn't mean anything by that, sorry, here I go again, putting my size tens in where they're not wanted."

"Size ten, eh? My, what big feet you have." She chuckled, finished the final mouthful of her dinner and pushed the plate to one side. "That was delicious, as always. I've never had a bad meal here, have you?"

"Never. I won't be long." He continued to tuck into his prime steak, enjoying the way it melted in his mouth with very little effort. He glanced up to see her studying him. His head tilted and he asked, "Is something wrong?"

"No, I'm just sitting here, trying to figure you out. I'm a people-watcher. I'm intrigued to know what lies beneath the outer layer of a person."

"I'm the same. Let's play a game, see what the other's perceptions are, okay?" She nodded and crossed her arms. "I'll go first, I see you as someone who has deep frustrations. Not only in your working life but also your personal life as well. What do I mean by frustrated? Well, you're desperate to see what life has to offer and sometimes, you fear taking the steps to achieve your dreams. How am I doing so far?"

Her eyes sparkled and her lips parted in a glimmer of a smile. "Maybe. Go on."

"Well, I can tell how determined you are to bide your time. You know that by being patient, the right opportunity is going to fall into your lap when you least expect it."

She unfolded her arms and clapped. "That's amazing." She dipped down and looked under the table and then sat upright. "I was just searching for your crystal ball."

It was his turn to laugh. "Never had one, I don't believe in that stuff, do you?"

"Sometimes. It depends how good the person is, there are so many fakes out there. In all walks of life."

"You speak the truth. It's your turn." He mimicked her by inclining his head and folding his arms, copying her to await her response.

"Hmm... let's see. You come across as someone who knows his own mind, maybe the fact that you run your own business is a telling sign on that front." He nodded. "You exude confidence, but beneath the skin, you're a little boy crying out to be loved."

He unfolded his arms, narrowed his eyes and pointed at her. "You're cheating, we've already established that I'm still grieving the loss of my parents."

"I am not. Even if your parents were still alive today, I believe I'd be saying the same thing. I've met men like you before, you're lacking the emotions that make you a whole person. Therefore, you spend most of the time putting on a false façade. The person you show to the world, although nice, isn't a true reflection of what lies beneath."

Wow! You've hit the nail on the head, baby, as you're about to find out later. "I hate to tell you that you've got it wrong, but truly, what you see is the true me. Yes, I'm grieving and possibly hurting inside, but I'm not afraid of showing it."

"Okay, I was wrong. Though in a way I was right."

"You were. Tell me what your aspirations are?"

"Mainly to find a soulmate who I can be happy with. I would want to explore the world together. Someone who hates arguing as much as I do. Go on, say it, I'm seeking the impossible, right?"

"Not at all. I hope you find the person you're searching for."

A mellow silence filled the gap between them as the waiter returned and whisked their plates away. "Would you care for dessert?"

"Layla?" Harvey asked.

"Oh, go on then. I can always spend an extra twenty minutes on the running machine at the gym tomorrow to compensate. I'll have the salted caramel profiteroles, please."

"That sounds divine. I'll have the same."

"Cream or ice cream?" the waiter asked.

"Ice cream," Layla said, cringing.

"The same for me, thanks."

The waiter left.

"How long have you worked at the solicitor's?"

"Around five years. I started working there when I was twenty-one."

"That's a long time, especially these days."

The conversation continued to flow for the next hour or so. Then, Harvey took a punt on hooking her inquisitive nature once more. "Do you like to fly? Or do you have an aversion to it?"

"I love flying. Detest the take-off and landing, like everyone else, but I really enjoy the bit in between."

He glanced at his watch, it was almost eight-thirty. "Have you ever seen Hereford and the surrounding area at night?"

She frowned. "No, I can't say I have. What are you suggesting?"

"I need to visit the gents, then I have a surprise for you, if you're up for it?"

"I'll contemplate that while you're in the loo."

He recognised the sparkle in her eyes that told him all he needed to know. Harvey left the table and went upstairs to the toilet. He fished his phone out of his pocket and typed out a text message to his brother.

. . .

Leaving the restaurant soon. Should be there within forty-five minutes, if everything goes according to plan. H.

His brother's response came back within a few seconds.

Plane is fuelled, ready for departure. High winds are forecast for later, so get a move on.

Harvey adored flying in adverse weather conditions, it added to the excitement. He returned to the table, adrenaline tearing through his veins at the prospect of what lay ahead. "Have you decided?"

"I think so. I'm going to give it a miss tonight. Maybe, if the offer is still on the table, we could go at the weekend. That is, if you still want to see me after I've rejected your proposal."

He pinned a smile in place, hoping to cover up his disappointment. "Of course. Whatever suits you. I'm thrilled there's a second date on the table, glad I haven't screwed things up by assuming you'd be up for a bit of adventure."

She paused and then smiled. "Go on, then. Let's do it tonight, why not?"

He punched the air and gathered her shawl off the chair as she got to her feet. He placed it around her shoulders and took the liberty of kissing her cheek. "You won't regret it," he whispered seductively.

"I'm excited beyond words. If you hadn't left me at the table to mull the proposition over, I would've rejected it out of hand. After all, I barely know you."

"Come now, you know enough about me to know that you can trust me. Let's get out of here. My pilot is ready and waiting."

She froze on the spot and stared at him. "What? How?"

He chuckled. "I was confident you would say yes and made the arrangements while I was in the toilet."

She laughed and led the way to the door. Harvey paid the bill before she could open her purse. "I know what we agreed, but please, have this one on me tonight. You can pay next time."

"See, that's your confidence shining through again. Okay, I agree. Thank you."

The cashier took the card payment, and they left the restaurant. "Did you come by car?" Harvey asked.

"No, by bus."

"Ah, that's great. My car is waiting for me around the corner."

They rounded the corner to find the limo parked at the kerb.

"No way. Is that yours?"

"Of course. I prefer to travel in style. Any objections?"

Her eyes widened. "None at all. It'll be my first time. How exciting, two thrills in a single night. How will you top this on the second date?" she giggled.

"I'm sure I'll think of something exceptional, I always do."

The chauffeur opened the back door and Harvey gestured for Layla to get in first, then he climbed in after her. She settled into her seat and surprised him by slipping her hand into his as she took in her plush surroundings.

"This is divine," she whispered.

He leaned over and gently brushed his lips over hers. "Only the best for you, Layla."

She smiled and rested her head on his shoulder. She remained in the same position until they reached the airfield. He exited the car and held out a hand for her to take, then led her up the steps to the plane.

"Wow! All this is yours?"

"It is. Here, take a seat, let's get you comfortable for the journey."

He supported her by the elbow and walked towards the executive chair. He lowered her into the chair and dipped under the table to collect the piece of rope he'd placed there earlier. She took one look at it and kicked him in the shin. She screamed, sensing what was about to happen, judging by the fear he read in her eyes.

"Hush now, no one can hear you. Be a good girl, don't make me mad. If I get mad, I'll end up hurting you."

"I don't want to go with you. I refuse to. She bounced out of the chair and shoved him backwards with a strength that caught him off-guard. She attempted to run towards the door, but he promptly regained his balance and pounced on her. Grabbing a handful of her hair, he tugged her. She screeched, swore several words a young lady should never spew out of her mouth and spun around to face him, her eyes blazing.

"Come on then, arsehole, show me what you've got. Sorry, did I forget to mention I'm a black belt in karate?"

His eyes narrowed, trying to figure out if she was telling the truth or not. She assumed the position, her knees bent, her slanted hands out in front of her, ready to chop at him.

He tipped his head back and laughed.

Aggrieved, she inched forward, toppling on her heels. He clenched his fist and with their gazes locked in defiance, he lashed out before she realised what was happening. She stumbled, dazed. "*Arsehole, am I? Well, little lady, I'm about to show you what this *arsehole* is capable of doing to a feisty bitch such as yourself.*"

Again, she recovered her composure and bounced back onto her feet, yelling as she flew at him. This time he was too quick for her and successfully stepped to the side before she could make contact. Layla ended up hitting the wall and rebounded back into his arms. He twisted her to face him; her forehead was split open. "You're going to regret doing that. You and I... we could've been good together, for a while anyway. Now, well, you've pissed me off and are about to suffer the consequences."

She surprised him by lashing out. Her fingernails ripped a deep gash into his left cheek. He grappled for her wrists and managed to secure them, then he slapped her a few times.

The door to the cockpit flew open. "What the fuck is going on, Harvey?"

"Daniel, help me, she's out of control."

Daniel came to his rescue, and between them, they suppressed her fighting spirit enough to tie her up.

"Okay, let's get out of here," Harvey suggested.

Daniel turned and closed the door behind him. Harvey hoisted the steps up himself and locked the outer door. He grinned as the spark of an idea coursed through his warped mind.

He returned to his seat and stared at Layla who now seemed resigned to her fate, tears dripping onto her cheeks. She whispered, "I'm sorry. I didn't mean to lash out. I'll do anything you want, just please, please untie me."

Harvey glared at her and shook his head. "What kind of fool do you fucking take me for, lady?"

Her eyes narrowed. "You'll be sorry. I know people in high places, you'd be wise to remember that."

"Look around you, bitch, and you think I don't? You think it costs a pittance to run this plane? My wealth is often seen as an influencer to others in business and everyday life."

"Ha, as if. You'll get your day in hell. I won't let this drop, you'd be foolish to think otherwise."

"We'll see. You're not going to be around long enough to do any damage to my enterprise. I have something very special planned for you, feisty lady."

"Such as?" she demanded, her defiance notching up the scale.

"You'll see soon enough. For now, enjoy the ride."

The plane taxied down the runway. He studied Layla carefully. She'd told him over dinner how much she feared the take-off during a flight. She closed her eyes, and her mouth moved now and again, as if she was muttering a silent prayer. Once the plane had levelled out, she opened her eyes and let out a relieved breath.

He smiled tautly. "See, nothing to worry about, was there?"

"Fuck off!"

"Now, now, is that any way to treat someone who is about to give you one of the biggest pleasures in your life?"

She frowned and asked, "What's that supposed to mean?"

"You'll see. Only a few more minutes now."

She glared at him again, an utterly intense stare that if he didn't have self-assurance gushing through his veins, might have unnerved him.

He waited a few more minutes and glanced out of the window at the lights below until there was only darkness beneath them. "Remember when I promised I'd show you the area at night? Well, you're about to see it first-hand, so to speak." Harvey yanked Layla by her bound hands to stand her upright. He was aware that her tied ankles would assist in restricting her movement. He flopped her over his shoulder and walked a few paces to the door of the plane.

He was a risk taker, he knew his brother would be pissed at what he was about to do, but fuck it, he had a need growing inside him that was crying out to be satisfied. He pushed the door open, and she screamed. He clung on tight to the rail and heaved Layla out of the plane. The plane dipped, first one way and then the other. Harvey grappled to find the door handle again, and after an intense struggle against the strong winds, managed to secure it in place once more. His gaze was drawn to the side window as he watched Layla's body tumble into the darkness below.

He ventured into the cockpit, prepared for his brother to rip into him.

"What the *fuck* did you do?" Daniel demanded, his hair damp, the sweat pouring from his forehead due to his exertion to keep the plane level.

"Let's just say I changed my mind. Didn't think she suited our purpose. On top of that, she was pissing me off, so I got rid of her." Harvey laughed and peered through the windscreen.

Daniel stared at him open-mouthed for a few seconds. "Jesus! You're fucking unpredictable! You've gone too far this time. That's it, I've had enough. You realise your demented behaviour could have killed us both, don't you?"

"The thought never even crossed my mind. These bitches need to know who the boss is. You know me, I refuse to take shit from any woman. Anyway, stop questioning my actions. Just fly the goddamn plane."

"Where do you want me to fly it, now you've dumped the fucking cargo we were carrying? Or hadn't you thought about that?"

"Turn around. I'll ring Mick to pick us up from the airfield. That's it, all sorted without me getting a hair out of place, as usual. Well, maybe that was a slight exaggeration." He laughed again and returned to the cabin to take his seat. The plane veered off to the right and descended a few minutes later. Harvey relived the moment he ditched Layla, literally, and grinned.

Nothing feels more satisfying than seeing fear in a woman's eyes just before she dies. I'm such an evil bastard!

9

Sara had to drag herself into the station on Saturday morning; six straight days on the trot were taking their toll on her body. Mark, bless him, insisted on getting up early to prepare her a breakfast of scrambled eggs and bacon. He was an absolute gem, and not for the first time, she felt fortunate to have him in her life. It was getting increasingly difficult to imagine a life without him. Her marriage to Philip was now a very long and distant memory, and it had been replaced by the joy of having Mark in her life. She hoped against hope that this time, her happiness was going to last forever.

The niggling that cropped up now and again hadn't gone unnoticed, leading her to wonder if she deserved to be this happy and content.

She parked her car and entered the station, surprised to see the regular desk sergeant on duty. "No rest for the wicked, eh, Jeff?"

"So it seems. One of the guys called in sick this morning, they rang me to replace him. I don't mind, I didn't have much on this weekend anyway. How come you're here, Ma'am?"

"This investigation has got under my skin. Can't stand the thought of two women being out there, scared shitless, fretting about what is likely going to happen to them."

"I can understand that. Any leads so far?"

"We've got a limo we need to track down, that's about it."

"There can't be that many in the area, can there? I wouldn't class Hereford as being affluent."

"Around fifty."

"Wow, really? I suppose that's more than enough for you and your team to try and trace."

The outer door opened and Carla walked in. Sara smiled and asked, "Hi, how are you on this dreary January Saturday?"

"Let's just say my mood is matching the weather today."

"Come on, I'll buy you a coffee. See you later, Jeff."

"Have a productive day, ladies."

"Fingers crossed for us," Sara called over her shoulder and hooked her arm through Carla's.

A few minutes later, Carla brought a coffee into her office. Sara glanced at her paperwork. "Should I have given my weekend up for this crap?"

"Why don't you leave it until Monday? No one will notice."

"I think I will. Is Craig here yet?"

"Yes, he's just shown up."

"I'll come and have my coffee with you two then, it can get lonely in here sometimes."

Carla nodded and retreated out of the room.

"Bloody hell!" Craig shouted.

Sara raced out of her office to join him. "What's up?"

"I put out an alert on the ANPR system before I left yesterday. I've just checked my emails and they contacted me early this morning. I should have checked first thing and forgot." He thumped his fist against his thigh.

"I won't have self-recriminations in this office, Craig, you know that."

"I know. Anyway, apparently, the limo was spotted last night in the centre of Hereford."

"What? Why wasn't uniform alerted and instructed to swoop on the driver?"

Craig winced. "I set up the wrong type of alert, boss. I only asked for an email to be sent to me. Damn, why didn't I check it earlier?"

"It still wouldn't have helped, Craig. Can you bring up the footage?"

"I can try. Give me a few minutes, I'll get back to you."

Sara paced the floor, her anxiety rising with every step, until Craig gestured for her to join him.

"Here it is. The driver is in the car, waiting for someone by the look of things."

"Interesting. Scroll forward."

Craig whizzed through the footage to around eight-thirty. They watched the driver get out of the limo and open the back door. Two people came into shot, a man in a suit and a young woman wearing an evening dress and shawl.

"Interesting. Can we get a close-up of the man, Craig?"

He zoomed in, but the picture was pixelated and very grainy. "Bugger, that's no help, is it?"

"Not at all," Carla agreed. "Shit! Does this mean another girl has gone missing?"

"Maybe, or she could be his permanent girlfriend. They seem pretty close, or is that my imagination? I'm just thinking how awkward I used to feel on a date if I didn't know the girl that well," Craig suggested.

"Possibly. The truth is, we can only speculate. Craig, maybe in time you can try to clear up the image a little? Perhaps we can check the restaurants in the area, see if we can find any better images of them. Might be worth a shot. For now, though, can you find out where they headed?"

"I can have a tinker with it." He fast forwarded the tape and the three of them observed in silence as the car left the city and picked up the A49.

Sara's heart sank. "Do your best to track it down, Craig, this could be the lead we've been waiting for."

"I'll try, leave it with me."

Sara and Carla backed away. "What do you want me to do?" Carla asked.

"We'll both look back over what we've got so far, not that there's much to hand at present, that's the ultimate frustration for me."

They settled down at Carla's desk and went through the list of clues they had uncovered so far. Half an hour into their deliberation, the phone in Sara's office rang. She bolted out of her chair to answer it. "DI Sara Ramsey, how—"

"Cut the speech, I haven't got time for that."

"Lorraine, is that you? Of course it is, what can I do for you?"

"Nothing. I'm contacting you to tell you I'm looking at a dead body."

"Right. What do you expect me to say to that?"

Lorraine sighed. "It's the body of a female, she's lying in a field out in Leominster. Do you want to attend, it's a weird one?"

"Weird? In what respect? I'm dealing with two missing person cases, I don't have time to fit a suspicious death into the mix, if that's what you're telling me."

"I'm not saying a word, other than I think you should attend this one. Are you up for taking my word?"

"Always. Okay, give me the location, Carla and I will be with you shortly."

Lorraine gave her the postcode she needed for the satnav and hung up.

"We'll be back shortly, Craig, keep up the good work."

"Good luck, boss."

*S*ara and Carla left the car. Carla stared down at her suede ankle boots. "Shit, these are going to get mucky as hell, if the field is boggy. I don't suppose you have a spare pair of wellies in there, do you?"

"I haven't. Even if I had, they probably wouldn't fit you. I'm only a size four and a half. You must be a size six at least."

"Spot on." Carla reached into the boot and extracted a pair of paper shoe covers. "I suppose these will offer your footwear some protection."

"They'll be better than nothing."

Sara smiled and reached back into the boot. "Let's chuck on a suit, just in case."

They slipped into a paper suit each and walked through the open gate to the field where a group of SOCOs and Lorraine were setting up their equipment.

"Hey, what have you got for us?" Sara called out when she was several feet away from the victim.

"Come and see for yourself. You took your time getting here," Lorraine chastised.

"Traffic was horrendous," Sara replied, hoping her tongue wouldn't swell up because of the white lie she had told. It hadn't taken them that long to travel the sixteen- or seventeen-mile journey to get there, not really.

Carla nudged her when the victim came into sight. "What the fuck?" Carla muttered.

"Shit! My eyes aren't deceiving me, are they?" Sara asked, shocked.

Carla shook her head and replied, "If they are, then mine are doing exactly the same."

"Do you mind telling me what you two are wittering on about?" Lorraine demanded, her arms crossed, tapping her foot in annoyance.

"We believe this girl was with a chap we're interested in tracking down. They were caught on camera in the city last night, then they left the area in a limo. The same limo connected to the missing person case we're working on," Sara said, her gaze still drawn to the victim.

"Ah, so my calling you out was justified after all, then. I just thought this case would be right up your street."

"You did right ringing me. What do you reckon happened? She got in the car with this bloke. I have to say, they seemed pretty comfortable in each other's company from what we could tell. He drove her out here and did away with her in this field? Or did he kill her in the car and dump the body here?"

Lorraine shook her head slowly and looked up at the sky.

"What?" Sara asked, confused.

"I'm taking a huge gamble on this one, but I think she fell from the sky."

"That's insane. How could that…?"

"I don't know. Let my guys finish taking the pics and then I'll show you what I mean. I had a sneaky peek at her earlier and was shocked at what I discovered, another reason for putting the call out to you."

They waited patiently for two photographers to fire off dozens of shots, after which they stepped back from the corpse. Lorraine got down on her knees and turned the body over. She pointed at the grass and mud beneath the woman's body. "I couldn't figure it out when we arrived. I saw the large indent in the soil beneath her. I've been wracking my brains, trying to consider different scenarios, and the only genuine suggestion I can come up with is that she fell from the sky. Another ten feet that way and she would have ended up in the centre of that big tree and probably remained undiscovered for weeks."

"You're kidding. All right, wrong thing to say, judging by your stern expression. But, this is unthinkable, Lorraine. How does a body fall from the sky?"

"I've seen it in books I've read for research purposes, it's not inconceivable."

"It's not? But how?"

"I believe the woman fell from either a plane or possibly a hot-air balloon, as unbelievable as that sounds."

"But how?"

"Stop asking the same damn question, Sara. I'm not the bloody oracle, all I can report are the facts as I find them. It's up to you to figure out the whys and wherefores. Sorry to be so arsy with you."

"It's okay, I'm used to it." Sara issued a toothy grin.

"Yeah, right."

"What do you suggest we do?"

"Oh great, as well as doing my fucking job, you want me to come up with something to make your life easier. You're looking at the wrong person if you expect that, love."

"All right. Get your hand from up your arse, I was only asking. Who found her?"

Lorraine pointed at a gentleman, standing by the gate on the other side of the field. "The owner of the land, the farmer. He's pretty shaken up, as you can imagine."

"Poor bloke. I'll have a word."

"You do that," Lorraine grumbled and returned her attention to the corpse.

"Before I go, any ID on her?"

"Nope."

"Was she interfered with? You know, raped?"

"My initial assessment says no. I'll give you a definitive answer later, after the PM."

Sara nodded and took a few paces, then looked down at how muddy the field was. "You stay here, Carla. I'll do this one."

"What do you want me to do?"

Sara contemplated the question. "Ring Craig, get him to check the flight paths in this area."

"You seriously think she came from a plane?" Carla asked, incredulity prominent on her face as well as in her tone.

"Hard to believe, but if that's what Lorraine is indicating, then we have to follow that line of thinking, otherwise we've got nothing."

"Okay. Maybe there's an airfield around here. I can't think of one off the top of my head, but then, the need to know that information has never surfaced before."

"Get on it. I'm newish to the area, so I haven't got a clue either. I'll be back soon. Why don't you go back to the car? It'll be warmer and more comfortable for you."

Carla grinned. "That's what I love the most about working with you, boss, your thoughtfulness."

"Shoo... Stop mocking me."

The farmer stared at her as she approached him. "Hello, sir. I'm DI Sara Ramsey and you are?"

"Dick Pullman. I own this land, for my sins. Terrible to come across something like this in the morning. Not what one expects to stumble across in his field. Do you know who she is?"

"I'm sorry you were the one who discovered the body. We're at a loss to know who the victim is, as there was no ID found on her. This may be a silly question, but I don't suppose you recognise her as being a local, do you?"

"No, I don't," he replied, indignantly. "Was she raped and dumped here? I couldn't bear the thought of that. I have a granddaughter around her age." He shook his head in disgust.

"We don't believe so. Try not to upset yourself, I know that's easier said than done." Sara paused a beat before she asked the next question, "I don't suppose you heard a plane flying overhead last night?"

He frowned and stroked the grey whiskers covering his chin. "A plane... no, you don't think she fell out of a plane, do you? Well, I've heard some crazy suggestions in my seventy years on this earth, but that has to take the bloody biscuit, that does."

"We're not sure. We have to cover all possibilities at this stage. Did you hear anything, either last night or this morning?"

He stared off behind her as he thought. "Nope, I don't think I did. Although, saying that, once I'm at home, the TV tends to be up loud because my wife is deaf. I've told her umpteen times to get her damn ears tested." He poked a finger in his right ear and waggled it. "Makes my head ring, it does. No doubt I'll be as deaf as her one of these days."

"Sorry to hear that, sir. What about this morning?"

"Nothing untoward happened, not that I can put a finger on anyway, sorry. Hard to believe she fell from the sky though, if that's what you're implying."

"It's a genuine possibility at this stage. Where is your farmhouse located?"

He pointed to the west of them. "A couple of fields over that way."

"Okay, so you wouldn't likely hear a vehicle if it stopped in the lane where my car is parked?"

"No. I'd have to have a bionic implant for me to hear something as far away as that."

Sara was at a loss what to ask next. Instead, she dug out a business card from her jacket pocket and handed it to him. "If you should think of anything else I should know about, feel free to contact me on that number."

He stared at the card and shrugged. "Is that it?"

"It's all we have at the moment. If you neither heard a plane nor a vehicle in the vicinity, then I need to get on with my investigation and find someone who did, sir."

"Ah, I see. Off to check with the neighbours, see if they heard anything, is that it?"

"That was my intention, yes. Are there many in the area?"

"This is a farming community. Four farms including this one, some small and some as big as this. I dare say someone might have heard something that I missed. Sorry to have let you down."

Sara smiled to reassure him. "You haven't, not in the slightest. I'll be off, then. Take care, Mr Pullman."

"I will. I hope you solve the mystery. I suppose I'll read about it in the papers, will I?"

"Maybe, if we ever solve the crime." Sara returned to the car, but stopped off to speak to Lorraine on the way. "Anything else for me? If not, we're going to knock on a few doors in the area, they're few and far between, apparently."

"Nothing more from me, not until I've cut her open."

"Too much information. I'll speak to you soon."

"You will that. Let me know if you find out whether my theory is correct."

"I will, don't worry."

Sara dodged the huge cow pats on the way back to the car and slipped off the shoe covers before she got in the vehicle. Carla was still on the phone, and she listened in on the conversation.

"Okay, that's all for now, Craig. We'll be back soon. Do your best. That's all any of us can do at this stage." Carla jabbed the End Call button.

"What did he say?"

"After he picked his chin up off the floor, he told me there's an airfield in the area at Leominster. He's given me the address, if you want to check it out."

Sara inserted her key in the ignition and kicked the engine into life. "We have a busy morning ahead of us, looks like our coming into work today has been justified already."

"Are you sure you're not some kind of witch? Or psychic? Did you know something like this was about to happen today?"

"Did I fuck. Right, let's get cracking."

"What first?"

"Knocking on the doors, in the hope someone can corroborate hearing a plane in the area."

The first farmer they questioned was reluctant to speak to them. He was a withered old man who walked with a cane and barely heard what Sara asked him, even though she shouted her questions.

They gave up trying and moved on to the second farm. The door was opened by a friendly lady in her early fifties. "Hello, how can I help?"

Sara produced her ID and stated the reason they were there. "I don't suppose you heard a plane flying around the area either last night or early this morning, did you?"

"Why yes, yes I did. It was around nine, maybe nine-fifteen last night. Hubby came in, said he'd seen it while he was checking on the cows in the barn, bedding them down for the night."

"Excellent news. Can you tell us anything else about the plane?"

"Not really, dear. It sounded like an annoying fly to me. No, wait, hubby came in and said he'd heard the engine struggling a bit at some point. He rushed outside because he feared it was going to come down on the barn."

"Interesting. Was it flying low then, is that what you're saying?"

"Why don't I call hubby to speak to you? Come inside, out of the cold. I was just about to pop the kettle on, fancy a brew? I'm Maureen by the way."

"Sounds wonderful, any chance of a coffee?" Sara asked.

"I'm sure we have some in the back of the cupboard. Come through."

Sara and Carla followed the woman into a very dated kitchen that was heated by an Aga, chucking out an obscene amount of heat.

"Take a seat. I'll ring Bob, see if he can spare you a few minutes. He's out there, tending the cattle, should be due back soon, so don't go thinking you're putting him out, you're not. We always have a cuppa around now, anyway." The back door opened before she had the chance to pick up the phone. "Ah, there you are, Bob. We have visitors."

"I can see that," he grumbled. He took out a pouch of tobacco and started rolling a cigarette. "Who are ye, and what do ye want from us?"

"They're the police, love. They're here about that plane we heard last night. I was just about to call you. Can you tell them what you heard and saw?"

"Can't say it was much. Thought the darn thing was going to come down on the bloody barn. There was a strange noise coming from the engine, then it appeared to right itself. What was a plane doing going out at that time of night if there was a problem with it? That's what I want to know. People need to have more sense than to fly when it's pitch black. Now, don't you go expecting me to give you any more than that because I have nothing. Why do you want to know?"

Sara smiled at the man who continued to roll his cigarette. "One of your neighbours discovered a body in his field this morning. Our pathologist believes the victim came from a plane, hence our enquiries."

"Well, bugger me. Is that right? Jesus, it couldn't have been the pilot, otherwise the darn thing would have come down. Which neighbour?"

"Mr Pullman."

"Oh shit! Poor Dick, I hope he's okay? He's got a dodgy ticker, needs to take more care of himself, he does."

"He seemed fine when we left. Maybe you can drop by later, make sure he's okay."

He tapped his forehead. "I've already thought about that. I don't need no copper telling me what to do with regard to my neighbour's welfare, thanks very much."

His wife slapped his arm, almost knocking the tobacco off the paper. "Now, Bob, you apologise this instant. That comment was uncalled for."

Sara raised a hand. "It's fine. We have broad shoulders."

The kettle boiled and the farmer's wife made the drinks.

"Is there anything else you can tell us, Bob?" Sara asked. She prepared herself for getting her head bitten off again, but the farmer surprised her.

"No, nothing that I can think of. I thought it strange that the plane should fly overhead. Actually, now that I think about it, we've had a lot of activity with planes flying over this week. I know we're close to the airfield, but we can usually count the number of planes we hear fly past on one hand over the course of the month. Ain't that right, Mo?"

His wife nodded, slowly at first until her head gathered momentum. "I never thought about it. Now that you've mentioned it, I can count at least three times we've heard a plane nearby this week."

Carla jotted down the information. "That's interesting," Sara stated. "I don't suppose you can remember which days?"

"I can't, not off the top of my head. What about you, Bob?"

"Monday, I seem to recall. It was earlier though, much earlier. I'm inclined to say it was during the day."

"In the morning or afternoon?"

Bob scratched the side of his head and then lit his cigarette. "Late morning going on towards lunchtime, does that help?"

"It does. See, you've been super helpful already. Any other time you can think about?"

The husband and wife both shook their heads. "No, sorry," Mo replied.

Sara thanked the couple. She and Carla downed the rest of their coffees and left the farm soon after.

They drove to the final farm in the area, but there was no response when they knocked on the door. "We'll leave it for now, I think we have enough to be going on with."

"Over to the airfield, then?"

"Correct. Let's get this out of the way and maybe we can stop by our favourite place, Queenswood Café. We could pick up a takeaway, take one back for Craig as well. We can reheat it in the microwave once we get back to the station."

"Sounds good to me. My tummy has started rumbling already at the thought of having one of their chicken burgers and chips."

"Easy girl. We have another visit to make first."

"I know, but you mentioned food and my stomach reacted."

Sara chuckled. "Soon, I promise."

The airfield was out in the middle of nowhere. *Fair enough, even if it's small and not very busy, it makes sense to locate it out here.*

They exited the car and walked towards the building with the reception sign over the door. A young man with slicked back hair and a friendly face smiled at them as they entered. "Hello, how can I help?" He tidied up a pile of papers and set them aside in an orange in-tray. Then, he approached the wooden reception desk.

Sara and Carla flashed their IDs. "DI Sara Ramsey and this is my partner, DS Carla Jameson. We're here to make enquiries about a plane which possibly took off from here last night."

He frowned. "You are? May I ask why? I'm Terry Ford, by the way."

"We believe it is connected to a serious crime."

His head shot back and his eyes widened. "Serious crime?"

"Yes, I can't reveal what that consists of at this time. Did a plane take off from here last night?"

He reached for a large book on his left and flicked through it. "Yes. One of the smaller planes went out for around half an hour, a short trip for them."

Sara shot Carla a quick look and raised her eyebrow. *This could be the break we're looking for.* "Would you mind giving us some information about the flight?"

"Of course. What do you need to know? Wait, why don't we take a seat over there?" He pointed at a seated area off to the left.

Sara nodded and the three of them settled in the comfy chairs. Carla flipped open her notebook and poised her pen.

"We'd like to know who owns the plane."

He trotted back behind the counter and ran a finger through another book and called over, "Barrows Associates. They're regular flyers from this airfield and store their plane in one of the hangars."

The same people who arranged the interview with Amber. This has to be them. "I see. I don't suppose it would be possible to see that plane, would it?"

He hesitated. Then smiled. "I can show you the outside, can't let you aboard though, not without the relevant paperwork in place."

"I understand completely. Can you tell me how many times a week the plane is used?"

"Just recently it's been more frequent. They've used it three, maybe four times this week already. You said you believe it has been used in a major crime, can you enlighten me on that?"

"We believe someone might have been either thrown from the aircraft or they possibly jumped. Either way, we're dealing with a dead body."

He gasped. "No! Well, I never."

Sara scanned the area outside. "Do you have cameras on site?"

"You're going to hate me. I've had to put up dummy ones, funds are really tight and... go on, you can lecture me now. Kick my arse around the building a few times if you feel the need."

Sara sniggered. "It's unfortunate, your secret is safe with us. I suggest you rectify that in the future though, running an airfield comes with a significant responsibility. How sure can you be that unscrupulous people don't use this place to traffic drugs in and out of the county? It used to be rife at one stage in Hereford, so I've heard."

"God, don't tell me that. I'll get it actioned ASAP, I promise. I'll get a small business loan out if I have to. The thought of criminals using this airfield as their means to transport filthy drugs into the area is giving me the heebie-jeebies. The last thing I want is to be associated with people like that."

"Glad you're prepared to take your business more seriously now. My motto is trust no one, especially in business."

"That's a good motto to have. I would be wise to take a leaf out of your book."

"Do you track the flights of the aircraft?"

"Yes, I like to. What do you need to know? I'll get the appropriate ledger, and yes, I have a different ledger for every aspect of the business. Weird, I know. I get it from my father, actually. I took over the airfield when he sadly passed away a few years ago."

"Sorry to hear of your father's passing."

"Thanks. The business used to be far more profitable in his hands. He cut back on his outgoings a lot in order to make a sizeable profit every year. I'm struggling to emulate his success, and to be honest, some months I struggle to make ends meet. I've got no one to bounce ideas around with, I'm single, you see. No family to ease the burden of the stress."

"What about your mother?"

"She died when I was born. It was Dad and me against the world, until his passing. He did his best raising me as a single parent, I suppose."

"That's so sad. What about the Aviation Authority? Or the specific governing body, can't they give you any worthwhile advice?"

"I'm in contact with someone, but sadly, not getting the results I need to turn a profit. Anyway, you don't want to hear about my woes. What can I do to help you with regard to this plane?"

"What would really help is if you could supply us with a possible flight path the plane has taken this week."

"I think I can do that. Let me see. They have to log the mileage and give a reason for their trips. Yes, here we have it, Monday and Thursday, two separate trips to the same place."

"Which is where?"

"An airfield in the Shropshire Hills."

"And what reason was given?"

"A business meeting."

"Can you give us an address for the airfield?"

He read it out for Carla to jot down. Sara's adrenaline kicked up a notch, she could sense only good things would come from obtaining this information. She had high hopes it would lead them to where Amber was, maybe where Davina was, too. If the two girls were being kept together.

"I'm going to ask a really big favour of you now," Sara said, looking Terry in the eye, holding his gaze.

"Go on, if it is within my realms to help, I will."

"That's great news. I need you to ring me if someone from Barrow Associates logs the plane out again."

"Of course. I'll do that right away."

"Excellent. I think we're done here. We'll contact the other airfield to see if they can shed any light on things at their end. I can't thank you enough for helping us out like this, Terry, it could blow our investigation wide open."

"Umm… can I ask if the victim was male or female?"

"Female. Does it matter?"

He ran a hand through his short black hair. "No, it was stupid of me to ask. Oh my, that's awful. Glad I could be of service in some small way. I'll definitely contact you as and when anyone gets in touch to make a booking."

Sara and Carla rose from their seats. Terry opened the door and saw them to their cars. "Wait, did you want to see the aircraft? It's sitting in the hangar over there."

Sara smiled. "Thanks, that would be brilliant."

They followed him across the tarmac to a large hangar. He pulled open the door to reveal a small plane, although it was larger than Sara had imagined. She withdrew her phone and shot off some photos. "Thanks, we have everything we need for now, Terry."

He secured the doors once more and walked back to the car with them. Sara shook his hand. "We appreciate your openness and help, Terry."

"Totally my pleasure. I'm keen to work with the police to keep this business above board. I hope the information helps to solve your investigation."

"I'm sure it will. Speak soon, hopefully."

He waved her card. "As soon as I hear anything."

Sara drove away from the airfield and back down the country lane to the A49. "Bloody hell. This could be it, Carla. What do you reckon?"

"It adds up, the information definitely has legs. How are we going to trace the buggers? We already know that Barrows Associates is a false name."

"First of all, we need to think positively. Terry seems a decent chap, I think he's going to do all he can to assist us when the time comes."

"Let's hope he doesn't put himself in jeopardy in the process."

"That's a valid point, considering they've just upped the ante and become murderers. Right, let's get lunch organised tout suite and then get back to the station."

"One question, if I may?"

"Go for it."

"How are we going to ID these people? We've got a false name in the email, a false business name under which the plane is registered, and in the email as well, where does that leave us?"

"Hanging our hopes on Terry informing us when the plane gets booked out again. They'd have to do that in advance, wouldn't they?"

"I should think so. Still, I reckon we're in for a frustrating time all the same."

"Yep, I agree. We'll bounce some ideas around when we get back."

"I have a suggestion, if you want to hear it, not sure how you're going to react to it, though."

Sara wagged her finger. "If you're about to put yourself forward for an undercover role, don't even go there."

"I wasn't, but now you mention it…"

"No way. I don't think we need to entertain going down that route, Carla."

"Okay, what about holding another press conference, then?"

"And say what?"

"You have the perp on camera, hopefully Craig will have worked his magic on refining the photo by now, put it out there. Or do you not want to do that in case it backfires on us in some way?"

Sara heaved out a sigh. "Don't think it hasn't crossed my mind. The thing that's holding me back is whether it will do the women he's abducted more harm than good."

"It's a real dilemma, granted. Maybe we should make a pros and cons list when we get back to base."

Sara laughed. "That thought had crossed my mind as well. Right, here we are. What do you fancy?"

"Chicken burger and chips. Here's the money." Carla dipped into her small handbag but by the time she'd raised her head again, Sara had left the car. "Oi, come back here," she shouted out of the window.

Sara turned, grinning, and ran two pointed fingers in a V-sign against her nose. Carla grumbled some expletives and closed her window again.

Sara joined the small queue at the takeaway window. When it came to her turn, she ordered three portions of chips, two chicken burgers and a cheeseburger for Craig, unsure whether he'd appreciate the chicken variety or not. She paid by card and stepped back to wait for her order. Rather than stand around doing nothing, she decided to give Mark a call. "Hi, just checking in on my favourite husband."

He laughed. "Your *only* husband... ugh, sorry, dumb retort."

"Silly man. Stop walking on eggshells, Mark. You're my husband now. Have I told you lately how much I appreciate having you in my life?"

"At least once a day, but I never get bored with hearing it. Fill your boots."

"Cheeky sod. Where are you?"

"At your parents' house. Say hi, everyone."

"Hi, Sara, love. Sorry you couldn't be with us today," her mother shouted.

"I'm sorry for letting you down, Mum, it was out of necessity, I promise."

"Now, don't you go saying that. Needs must, as they say. It's lovely to have Mark all to ourselves for a change. And yes, we've been busy pumping him for information about your honeymoon."

Sara's cheeks warmed up at the thought. "Umm... don't you go digging too much, a girl likes a little privacy from her parents in that department, Mum."

"Oh my, I didn't mean in that respect. Oh Gosh, I'm sorry. Hush my mouth."

Her mother's flustering made her snigger. "Sorry, I was only teasing. I knew what you meant. Maybe we can all go back up to Scotland for a family holiday in the near future. It's a beautiful part of the world."

"That would be a wonderful idea. Rent a cottage by the sea somewhere."

"We'll sit down and make some plans for a break later on in the year. Make sure you work Mark well while he's there. How's Dad?"

"He's a little under the weather today, nothing that a bit of bed rest won't cure. Mark has offered to do all the little jobs we have outstanding in exchange for a hearty lunch."

"Always thinking of your stomach, eh, hubby? Talking of which, I have to go, my own lunch is ready. We're at Queenswood, picking up a takeaway."

"Go, don't let it get cold. What time will you be home tonight?"

"I'm hoping to get away by five, that's the plan. Depends on how the investigation goes. It took a different direction this morning."

"Oh?"

"Tell you later. Love you." She ended the call and grabbed the paper bag from the girl behind the counter. "Thanks, see you again soon."

"You're welcome. Enjoy."

Sara handed Carla the food once she was back in the car and put her foot down on the way back into town.

Craig was thankful to see them. "God, I'm starving, you must've read my mind." He tore open his lunch and began eating it immediately.

"Easy, you'll get an ulcer. Do you want a coffee to go with that?" Sara asked.

Craig took another big bite of his burger and with his mouth full, he said, "I'll get them. What happened out there?"

"We managed to speak to the guy who runs the airfield, nice chap. He told us that Barrows Associates own a plane and that it has made a number of trips from the airfield this week. Their destination is to another airfield in Shropshire. I need to get on to them as soon as I've filled my belly."

"That name keeps cropping up, doesn't it?" Craig stated.

"Yep, the company that doesn't exist," Sara confirmed. She took a large mouthful of her chicken burger and savoured the crisp crumb coating of the chicken fillet.

"Where do we go from here then?" Craig asked as he popped a chip, slathered in ketchup, into his mouth.

"I've instructed the guy at the airfield, Terry, to contact me as soon as someone from the firm books another flight."

"The victim, you genuinely think she was thrown from the plane?"

"According to Lorraine. My take is she was either pushed or she fell to her death, maybe she tried to escape. It's a long shot, but that's all I have right now."

"That scenario seems a bit extreme," Carla piped up. She wiped her mouth on a napkin and picked up another chip.

"It does. I'm open to suggestions if either of you have any. The only other step I can think of to get any kind of reaction is to go with Carla's idea of holding another press conference."

"I managed to refine the image," Craig replied.

"Brilliant news. It has to work. It's all we've got. The name of the company, which is false, and his image. Is it good enough to run through the system, Craig?"

"I can try. There's no point in me trying to locate the limo now, is there? Now that we've made the connection with the airfield."

"No, it will only be a waste of time. I think we've finally hit a wall for now, until Terry gives us the heads-up."

"That's bloody annoying, there must be something we can do."

Carla drummed the fingers of her free hand on the desk while she took another bite from her burger.

"I can't think of anything. Apart from searching the map in Shropshire for a possible location as to where this guy might be holding the girls."

Craig's eyes widened and he gulped. "What? Do you have any idea what size Shropshire is?"

"All right, it might have been a daft suggestion but…"

"It's all we've got," Carla finished off for her.

Sara shrugged. "Exactly. The airfield is near Church Stretton."

"I've driven through there a few times, there are some hilly parts on that stretch," Carla noted.

"Craig, can you get the map up for me? Transfer it to the screen so we can have a more in-depth look at the area."

He put his burger on one side, wiped his fingers on the napkin and tapped at the keyboard. Sara switched on the fifty-inch TV screen on the far side of the room and wheeled it closer to where they were sitting.

"There you go. Give me the nod when you want me to zoom in," Craig reached for his burger again.

Sara peered at the screen and shook her head. "I can't tell, it's going to be pointless searching, as you say, it's bloody vast." She vented her frustrations and kicked out at a nearby chair, sending it hurtling against the wall to her office.

"That isn't going to help," Carla grumbled.

"Ha, it made me feel better for the tiniest instant." Sara left the desk and went over to where Will usually sits. "Will had a list of the limo owners, didn't he? Ah, yes, here it is. She ran her finger down the list and shook her head. "I thought he may have missed the firm. Nope, it's not on here." Sara left the list on her colleague's desk and returned to her seat with a sinking feeling ripping her insides apart. "I don't know what else to suggest. What about you two?"

Carla shook her head and threw the remains of her meal in the bin beside her. "Nothing."

Craig shook his head. "Me neither."

"Which leaves us with one other option on the table."

"Holding another press conference," Carla filled in the blanks. "You'd be within your rights, now that we have another girl reported missing, plus a victim we've yet to identify."

Sara rushed into her office to call Jane Donaldson.

"Jane, I know it's Saturday, I'm sorry to disturb you, but it's an emergency, I promise."

"Go on, what do you need?"

"Another press conference ASAP."

"At the weekend? I doubt we'd get many interested journalists, to be honest, Sara. Can't it wait until Monday?"

"I wish it could." She relayed the latest information they'd been working on to see if that would do the trick of jolting Jane into action.

It worked.

"All right. I have all my contacts in my phone. Let me see what I can organise from home and I'll get back to you in a little while."

"I owe you big time for this, Jane."

"Don't get carried away with yourself just yet."

"I won't. I know you'll do your best for me, though." Sara ended the call and returned to the incident room. "She's doubtful whether she can pull something together over the weekend, but she's going to pull out all the stops."

*T*en minutes later, Sara's office phone rang. She bolted into the room and answered it. "DI Sara—"

"It's me," Jane replied. "I've managed to secure you a slot for three this afternoon. It'll be a smaller audience than usual. I hope that's okay?"

"You're amazing. Smaller is fine, as long as the main players will be attending."

"They will. Local ITV and BBC TV plus a few of the heavy hitters from the paper world."

"I can't thank you enough for this, Jane."

"It didn't take that long to pull together, once I told them what the conference would be about."

"Gagging for it in the end, were they?" Sara chuckled.

"Definitely. Can you handle it on your own or do you need me to come in and deal with it?"

"No. The team and I have it covered. Sincerely, thanks so much, Jane."

"I'll be watching with interest when it airs this evening."

"I hope I can pull it off without your expertise to guide me."

"I'm not even going to answer that. Have faith in yourself. Good luck. I'm getting back to my cuddles now… umm… with my pooch."

"Crikey, I had a dreadful feeling that I'd interrupted some real action. Enjoy the rest of your day and thanks again, Jane."

10

---

*H*arvey was bored and out on the prowl. He'd fallen out with Daniel over the mishap which had happened the night before, when Layla had exited the plane before it landed. She'd pissed him off, she shouldn't have done that. Now, well, she was no longer around to matter.

That night, Daniel had stormed off the second the limo arrived back in Hereford. He'd ordered Mick to drop him off on the edge of town. He'd shouted that he'd rather walk the extra three miles home than share the same air with Harvey for a second longer. Harvey had shouted after him that he would call him in the morning. He'd tried, but Daniel was ignoring his calls. Rather than go around there to have it out with his twin, here he was, on the lookout for yet another victim.

As the evening drew in, he drove around the city, even more livid than he was earlier after hearing that daft cow on the news. DI Sara Ramsey… what he wouldn't give to wipe the smug smile off her face. He could sense the beam in her voice when she announced they had identified a suspect who they wished to speak to 'to help them with their enquiries'. He laughed, although another emotion soon developed. His anxiety levels notched up. He knew he was taking a risk being out and about, but he had a need to satisfy that dwarfed his anxiety.

Taking the main road out of Hereford towards Worcester, the A4103, it wasn't long before he stumbled across a young woman whose car had broken down. Being the gentleman that he was, he pulled over to offer her some assistance.

"Hi, let's see if I can help. What appears to be the problem?"

"Oh, hi, thanks for stopping. She just died on me and yes, before you say it, there is petrol in the tank. She's almost full."

"Okay, let me have a look under the bonnet." In truth, as convincing as he sounded, he didn't have a clue what to look for; he was the type of guy who drove a car but left the maintenance up to the experts to sort out. He made the right noises as he prodded and poked around with a few of the wires. After a couple of minutes, he stepped back and shrugged. "It's beyond me. I'm usually a dab hand with all things to do with all things engine related, but this has me flummoxed. Why don't I give you a lift to the nearest garage, see if anyone can assist you there?"

"Would you? Oh, wait, wouldn't it be better if you towed the car for me?"

"It would, except I don't possess a tow rope. Have you got one?"

Disappointment filled her features and she shook her head. "I haven't. I do have breakdown cover, maybe I would be better off ringing them instead. Yes, that's what I'll do. I appreciate you trying to help though, I truly do."

"Good idea. What about if I wait around with you? I hate the thought of leaving you all alone out here when it's getting dark."

The young woman smiled and offered her hand for him to shake. "Deal. I'm Nicola, by the way."

"Pleased to meet you, Nicola, I'm Harvey."

They climbed in the car and she made the call. He listened to her end of the conversation, her irritation increasing the more she was left waiting for someone to answer her damn call. He remained patient for a while and then said, "Maybe my idea would be better. In my experience, these breakdown companies are a waste of time at the weekend."

She sighed heavily. "I think you might be right. Go on, then. I'll lock the car up and join you in a tick."

He smiled and left the car. Adrenaline searing his veins, he jumped into the driver's seat and watched as she locked up her vehicle and trotted to join him.

"Thanks for being an utter hero. Not sure what I would've done if you hadn't come along. I hope the garage is still open."

"It should be. We'll soon find out. Buckle up."

Harvey started the engine, and she rested her head back; he sensed the tension of the situation easing during the drive. He spotted the garage up ahead and took a sideways glance. Her eyes were closed. He drove straight past and indicated into the road opposite, yet she didn't even stir. He slowed down and pulled into the next lay-by.

Nicola looked forward at her surroundings and then faced him. "I must have dropped off for a second. Where's the garage?"

"It was closed. I thought I'd pull in and reassess our options."

"Oh, what do you suggest?"

"Where do you live?"

"On the Bromyard Road in a small village you've probably never even heard of."

"I can drive you home and see if your husband can come and collect it."

She shook her head. "No, I don't have a significant other at the moment. I've just gone through a painful separation with an ex-boyfriend."

"Oh no, sorry to hear that. Did he cheat on you?"

She swallowed and faced him. "Yes, just like every other man I've ever been out with. He said it wasn't working between us. I followed him one night, and he met up with his tart. I struck out at both of them. I couldn't help myself."

He cocked an eyebrow. *She has a temper. I need to be wary here.* "I don't blame you. I probably would have done the same."

She glanced at the clock. "Shit! It's my dad's birthday. I'm due at his place in an hour or so. Would it be an imposition for you to drop me off at home? I'll have to worry about the car another time. I need to get to my parents' house, he's having a celebratory dinner for the family."

Aware that he didn't have much time, he decided it was now or never to make a play for her. His erection was already straining his zip. "Of course." He ran a hand up her leg. "Do you have time for a bit of fun first?"

"What? No. Get your fucking hands off me."

Seeing her refusal as the ultimate challenge, he upped his game. His fist came out of nowhere and knocked her out. His gaze roamed her body for a second or two, thoughts of what he was about to do playing like a movie in his mind. After a moment's pause, he unzipped his trousers and tore at the layers of her clothes, gasping and leering when he scooped her pert, rounded breasts out of her bra. Not caring where they were, he took advantage of her. Checking around him, to make sure no other cars were approaching, he lifted her out of the passenger seat and bundled her into the boot of the car. He bound her mouth with a piece of rag and tied her ankles and wrists together, then slammed down the lid.

He upped the music, satisfied by his latest acquisition. One more girl and the deal could be made. He tried calling his brother on his way home. Daniel was still refusing to answer his calls. *Damn! I need you, bro, don't frigging let me down now, not at this late stage in the game.* There were no other options left open to him, he would have to take her back to his place. Keep her there for now, until he and his brother were back on speaking terms, whenever that was likely to be.

When he arrived, he backed the car tight up to his garage door. He waited a few minutes to make sure none of his nosey neighbours were alerted to him being home, then he hauled Nicola's body into the house. He took her upstairs to the spare room and threw her on the bed. She was still out cold.

His mobile rang. He left the bedroom to answer it. "Daniel, hi."

"Don't fucking hi me, you bloody tosser. Have you seen the news? Your face is plastered all over it. You need to go to ground and quickly."

"Umm... shit! I can't."

"What? Why?"

"I've picked up another girl. I've been trying to call you all day. You ignored my calls so—"

"So? What, you're saying I'm the reason you've bloody kidnapped another girl? Sod you, bro. I told you, I've had enough of this shit. This is your problem now, I want nothing more to do with it, or you."

"Jesus, don't say that. What about the deal?"

"What about it? You think Mum and Dad are going to be pleased seeing you on TV, being linked with these crimes? You're deluded, man. Get a frigging life for fuck's sake."

"You're the only one who can fly the plane. I need you."

"Screw you. Get another mug to fly you. I'm done. D-O-N-E. Got that?" Daniel ended the call, leaving him dumbstruck and angry.

He paced the landing, his thoughts wildly spinning off in different directions. He had a few days left to make the drop and he couldn't handle the girls alone, he needed an accomplice. No, what he needed was to get his brother back on board.

Harvey returned to the bedroom. It was imperative he got out of there, before one of the neighbours rang the police. Maybe they'd already done that and the police were en route to his place. *Shit! Get a move on.*

He hoisted Nicola onto his shoulder and left the house. He popped the boot open and slung the woman into it. Then, he tore out of his drive and got on the road. *Where shall I go?*

He stumbled across the answer quickly. He checked his petrol gauge and put his foot down, deciding there was only one option left open to him. He would drive the girl to the cottage in Shropshire, not ideal—it would take him a good hour to get there, but it was the only solution he could come up with at such short notice.

11

---

ara, Carla and Craig were all excited to see the appeal go out, and they were surprised when the phones started ringing almost instantly with possible names. There was a mixture of names, but three people gave them the same one.

"Harvey Burrows keeps cropping up," Carla noticed. She wrote it on the whiteboard and circled it a few times.

"Wait! That's similar to one of the names on the limo list," Craig pointed out.

"Shit! You're right." Sara snatched the list off Will's desk, and her gaze was immediately drawn to Henry Barrows. She groaned, "It's too much of a coincidence, right? I should have made the connection sooner, Barrows Associates."

The phone rang again. Carla did the honours and answered it. She stared at Sara, her eyes wide open. "Can I ask you to hold the line for a moment, Miss Shaw?" She covered the mouthpiece with her hand. "This woman says she's Harvey Burrows' former girlfriend, says she has some information for us, but doesn't want to tell us over the phone."

"Okay, get her address, we'll shoot over there now." It was almost six-fifteen, so much for telling Mark she would be leaving around five.

She made a mental note to call him on the way to the woman's house. "Craig, are you okay to work longer?"

He waved a hand. "Sure. I'm enjoying myself, why would I want to go home?"

Sara chuckled. "Fair enough."

Carla ended the call and stood up. "She's out at Bobblestock."

"Let's go. I'm dying to hear what she has to tell us."

They set off, and en route, she rang Mark. He wasn't angry with her at all for going back on her word, not that she had expected him to be. "I'll see you later. We've got to stick with it now, love, I'm sensing we're closing in on the bastard."

"You've got to do what you think best, Sara. Just be careful out there. Come home in one piece."

She giggled. "I'm going to do my very best. See you later." She jabbed the End Call button.

"He's a good man, Sara. You've got a gem and a half there."

Sara briefly glanced sideways at her partner and patted her on the knee before returning her attention to the road ahead. "You'll find your own knight in shining armour soon, hon."

Carla sighed. "I think I'd rather stay single. Less hassle that way."

"Answer me one thing, do you believe Gary was behind the attack?"

"Truthfully? I don't think so. I doubt he'd have it in him to either pounce on me or get someone else to do it on his behalf. I'm intrigued to know who did, though."

"I haven't forgotten about it, I promise. Let's get this case out of the way and we'll throw some resources at finding your attacker next."

"I'm fine, don't worry about me. It was a minor blip which has taught me to be more wary regarding my surroundings in the dark."

"That's so wrong. You shouldn't need to go through life checking over your shoulder, expecting something to happen."

"I know, but what's the answer?"

"We'll find them, rough them up a bit before we haul their arses into the station."

Carla laughed. "You're hysterical when you're riled up."

"Thanks, although I was trying to be assertive. What number was it again?"

"Fifty-three. It's the one with the red door."

Sara parked the car and they exited the vehicle. The house, a neat little semi-detached, stood out like a beacon in the dark. "How to drain the national grid within one household."

Carla sniggered.

Sara withdrew her warrant card from her pocket and knocked on the door. A woman in her late fifties opened it and gestured for them to step inside. "Come in, come in. Elizabeth is waiting for you in the sitting room."

"Don't you want to check our IDs first?"

"If you insist." She nodded once she'd viewed their warrant cards and urged them to enter.

They followed her through the house to a large lounge at the rear. A young woman sitting in a wheelchair greeted them with an awkward smile.

"Are you Elizabeth Shaw?" Sara asked.

"Yes, that's right. Are you the officers dealing with the missing person cases?"

"Yes, I'm DI Sara Ramsey and this is my partner, DS Carla Jameson."

"Please, take a seat. I'm very nervous about speaking to you, but I think it's a necessity."

Sara and Carla sat on the sofa opposite the young woman. "We're so glad you called us. Perhaps you can tell us what you know about Harvey Burrows?"

"I intend to. There's a lot to tell you. Mum, would you make the officers a drink, please?"

"Of course. Sorry, I should have asked. What would you like?"

"Two coffees, milk, one sugar would be great, if it's not putting you out."

"It's not. I'll be right back." She cast her daughter a worried glance and reluctantly left the room.

Once the door was closed, Elizabeth let out a relieved sigh. "She smothers me at times. I know she's only looking out for me, but it's still a struggle all the same."

"I'm sure her intentions are good."

"They are. Anyway, you don't want to hear about my dull existence. Where do I start?"

"At the beginning would be best. You said you're the former girl-friend of Harvey's, how long did you go out with him?"

"Over two years. I suppose you could say I know him well. Him and his brother, Daniel, not sure if you're aware of this or not, but they're twins."

Carla jotted the information down and glanced up at Sara who was looking her way with her eyebrow raised.

"Twins? Are they identical?" Sara asked.

"No, far from it. Even in nature. Harvey is a go-getter in life. When he sets his mind on something, he goes after it with gusto."

"I see… and Daniel, does he try to hold his brother back?"

"Not really. Most of the time, he takes a back seat and lets Harvey get on with things. Every now and again, when he believes his brother has gone too far, he'll snap and cut him off for a few days, until Harvey backs down and apologises. I find it hard to believe that Harvey is connected with the missing person cases we've been hearing about on the news all week. Saying that, I shouldn't really be surprised, not when I cast my mind back to how he treated me."

"If it's not too upsetting for you, would you mind telling us how you got together?"

"I used to work at a gym in town. I can see the confusion written on your face. I wasn't always in a wheelchair, it's only been in the last two years…" She swiftly wiped away a stray tear and cleared her throat. "I refuse to get upset. I'm over it, over him."

"If you want to take a break at any time, please do. We've got all the time in the world, there's no rush."

"No, it's important for me to tell you this. I need to do it, if only to give me peace of mind. I've been struggling to find any of that lately, stuck in this thing."

Sara smiled. "It must be a tough situation for you to get used to."

"Some days are better than others. The winter mornings are the worst, the weather has a major affect on my joints, and I spend most days trembling, trying hard to keep warm. The doctor says it's all in my head, or words to that effect. It's all down to the accident, you see."

"What accident? Do you have it in you to tell us what happened?"

The door opened, and Elizabeth's mother entered the room. She set a tray down on the coffee table and retraced her steps to close the door. Then, she distributed the mugs and sat in the easy chair close to her daughter. "Have I missed anything? Have you told them what that bastard did to you?"

"Mum! Let it go. What's done is done. There's no turning back the clock, you know that." Elizabeth rubbed her mother's arm.

"He should have been punished, love. It's not right that he should be walking the streets after what he did to you. He stole your life, your independence."

Sara stared at the exchange between the two women; her curiosity heightened, but she held back, not wishing to interrupt.

"It's all right, Mum. We're coping, aren't we?"

Her mother tugged a tissue from the box beside her and dabbed at her eyes. "Yes, but life as we knew it is long gone now. He should have been punished... instead..."

"Leave it, Mum. There's no point going round in circles about this. I'm fine, I'm alive, that's all that matters."

"But at what cost?"

Elizabeth stared at her mother, and neither of them spoke for a few moments. "I need to speak to the officers, they don't want to hear this, Mum."

"Very well. In other words, 'sit here and shut my mouth' is that it?"

Elizabeth smiled at her mother. "You've got it in one. Sorry about that. Sometimes, the raw emotions emerge when we least expect them."

Sara smiled. "It's fine. By listening to your conversation, am I right in assuming that Harvey caused your disability?"

Elizabeth's chin dipped to rest on her chest. She raised it again, and Sara saw the unshed tears welling up. "Yes. Of course, he denies it, but

156

yes, he did this to me. The surgeon told me that I'm lucky to be alive. Sometimes, I wish I'd never survived."

Her mother gasped. "Elizabeth! Please, don't say that. I can't imagine life without you here."

"It's a fact, Mum. I keep strong most days because I'm afraid of upsetting you."

Her mother broke down. Elizabeth glanced at Sara and Carla and shrugged. She mouthed she was sorry and Sara smiled, letting her know that everything was okay.

"I do my best for you, Elizabeth. Your disability has turned both our lives upside down, not just yours. But I will never give up on you, no matter how much you try to push me away, and you do at times, believe me."

"I'm sorry, Mum. I don't mean to. I have days when I recall what my life used to be like. The fun I used to have going on walking expeditions with my friends."

"The same friends who have deserted you since the accident," her mother stated with another sniffle.

Elizabeth gulped. "Thanks for the unwelcome reminder."

"Oh gosh, I didn't mean to upset you. I'll keep quiet."

"Is that a promise?" Elizabeth asked, a glimmer of a smile tugging at her lips.

Her mother bowed her head in shame.

Sara sucked in a deep breath. "Would it be too hard, for both of you, if you explained how the accident happened?"

"Not for me. I can't change history. I'm stuck with the consequences, but life goes on, for all of us." Elizabeth shrugged and sighed a little and then added, "Harvey and I went on a walking holiday to West Wales, to Pembrokeshire. We were having a marvellous adventure, discovering the extensive coastline in that area." She smiled a little at the memory. "We rented a cottage close to the sea, so we had the exceptional walks nearby and were able to take off at will. Well, this particular day, Harvey had got up in a foul mood. I told him the walk would do him some good, it's surprising how invigorating a bracing walk by the sea can be, blows the cobwebs away, usually." She paused to sweep back a lock of hair. "Anyway, he agreed, but during the five-mile walk, his mood didn't alter at all, not in the slightest. I tried to draw him out of what appeared to be a depression, but it was as if he was revelling in being in a foul mood, if that makes sense. In the end, I walked on ahead, there was no way I was going to let him upset me and put a downer on the fabulous walk. He let me get a few hundred yards ahead of him, and the next thing I knew, he was standing beside me. I asked him if he was all right. He nodded, didn't speak and just stared at me. I chose to ignore him, thinking that he'd share what was bothering him, eventually. I wasn't about to let him spoil my day. The scenery in that particular area was breathtaking. I stood on the headland and stared out at the stunning coastline off to the left and to the right. Suddenly…" Elizabeth paused, gulped and stared off at the wall behind Sara.

"If it's too much, please, don't put yourself through the agony of telling us all the details."

"No, I have to. Every now and then, I need to voice how my disability occurred. Somehow it makes life bearable again for a few months. I know some people find that incredibly hard to believe, but it's true." Her gaze drifted over to her mother and she reached for her hand. "As I was saying, suddenly, I felt a hand in my back and the next moment, I was falling down the cliff face. My mind whirling as fast as I was travelling. Fear enveloped me and I grappled, trying to grab hold of some vegetation jutting out of the rocks, but there was nothing. You know what they say about life flashing before your eyes, it's true. I struggled to find anything. I ended up praying that something would break my fall. No sooner had the thought occurred to me, I came to a grinding halt when I landed on a ledge. I heard Harvey crying out for help. I can't tell you if he'd been shouting before I came to a halt or not, that's still fuzzy in my mind. I suspect he hadn't. Truth be told, he was watching my fall with a sinister sneer etched into his features."

What the fuck? Incredulity swept through Sara. "Really? You're convinced he pushed you and you didn't just lose your footing on the edge?"

"I'm positive that was the case."

"What happened next?"

"The rescuers came, thank goodness. One of them abseiled down the cliff face with a stretcher and I was pulled up to the top again. Harvey was all over me. Crying, kissing my face. I couldn't move, it was impossible to pull away from his false concern. I knew then that I had suffered serious damage to either my back or my neck. As it turned out, my neck was broken." She glanced down at the wheelchair. "And this is the result. I'm going to be forced to spend the rest of my life in this damn chair."

"I'm sorry to hear that, Elizabeth. Maybe the doctors will come up with a cure for your condition soon. Or am I talking baloney?"

Elizabeth smiled. "We're always hopeful, Mum, aren't we?"

"We are, love. We have to believe that, one day, a miracle might come our way."

Sara's heart went out to the young woman and her mother. She couldn't imagine the heartbreak the couple had gone through to get this far. "And Harvey? Did you complain to the police?"

"Oh, yes. He was arrested and the case went to court. The police believed me."

"That's great news. I'm sensing things didn't go as planned."

"That's right. His family is mega-rich, you see. They employed the services of a top barrister. There was no sympathy for me when he got me on the stand. He let rip, demoralised me and made me out to be a bloody liar."

"How awful, after all you'd been through, to be confronted with such callous behaviour."

"It rocked my world. Harvey got off on a technicality. Outside the courthouse, he and his family stood around, laughing with the barrister as Mum and I wheeled past them. It was horrendous, one of the worst days in my life, apart from when I went head first over that edge, that is. It took me months to recover from the humiliation. Knocked my confidence. I had dark thoughts and was desperate to end my life. Mum had to hide my pills from me. I used to lie in bed at night and cry myself to sleep. At the time, I thought my quality of life stank, sometimes, I still think that way. But then, his face appears in my mind and my determination grows... I've just realised what I've said, this truly isn't me trying to get revenge. Harvey is definitely the man in that photo, I swear he is. I wouldn't deliberately try to set out to destroy someone else's life, unlike some I could mention."

"To put your mind at ease a little, we've had a few calls mentioning Harvey's name, so I have no doubt what you're telling us is the truth. Have you had any contact with him since the court case?"

"He pops up on my phone now and again with a text message, asking how I am."

Her mother gasped. "You never told me that, Elizabeth."

"Because I didn't want to upset you, Mum. It's fine. I ignore the messages. I refuse to get rid of my number before you suggest it."

"Very well, I won't suggest it then." Sara smiled. "All I can do is reassure you that we're closing in on him. We can't arrest him just yet, as we have to consider the girls he has abducted. But now that he's killed one of them, we're going to find him and put him under surveillance."

"I don't understand," Mrs Shaw said.

"If they arrest him now, Mum, the girls might die if he doesn't reveal the location where he's keeping them."

"Ah, yes, of course, silly me."

"That's right. You said he comes from a wealthy family, can you tell us a little about his background?"

"Yes, his mother and father own a stately home out near Ross-on-Wye, but they've always refused to give their sons handouts. Right from the time Harvey and Daniel left university, their parents told them they had to make their own way in this world."

"Okay. What job does Daniel do?"

"He's a financial advisor, they both are."

"In Hereford?"

"Yes, in the centre of the city. It's called Burrows Finances."

"Excellent news. Would I be pushing my luck if I asked you for Harvey's address?"

"Not at all." She reeled off his address and the road where his brother lived, but she fell short of supplying the house number for Daniel's home.

Sara's phone rang. "Sorry, will you excuse me a moment? Carla, can you see if Elizabeth can give us anything else, like where his parents live exactly? Maybe Harvey's car details? Thanks, I'll just take this in the hall."

"Go, I've got this," Carla shooed her out of the room.

Sara answered the phone quietly in the hallway. "Craig, what's up?"

"Umm... I've just received a worrying call from a concerned parent, boss."

"Concerned? Can you enlighten me as to why they should be concerned?"

"Actually, I've received two calls within minutes of each other that have piqued my interest."

"Go on, sounds promising."

"The first was from a woman who was crying, I had a problem making out what she was saying to begin with. I thought she was one of those crank callers, messing me about. Anyway, once I could hear her coherently, she told me the woman in the photo with the suspect is her daughter, at least, she thinks it's her."

Sara's heart leapt with interest, but then sank when she realised what that meant. She'd have to break the news to the woman that her daughter was lying in the mortuary. "Crap. Did she give you a name?"

"The mother's name is Helen Davis, her daughter's Layla Davis."

"Okay, I'll need her contact details in a second, no, wait, let's deal with them now." Sara jotted down the address for the woman and then returned to the reason Craig had initially called her. "And the concerned parent, what was that all about?"

"Ken Thompson rang up about his daughter, Nicola. He was expecting her to join him for his fiftieth birthday, but she hasn't shown up. He realises that he should wait twenty-four hours before reporting her missing, but wanted to ignore that, sensing that something is wrong and in light of the appeals that you've put out this week, well, he thinks it's something we should investigate ASAP."

"I agree with him. I'm going to ask you to deal with that, Craig, otherwise, it could be hours before I can get back to him. Get Nicola's car and phone details, do the necessary checks on both. We're going to be stretched with what we've got on our plate. They're going to hate me for this, but I think we should rally the troops. Nicola's dad isn't the only one who senses something is wrong."

"I'll ring the rest of the team now and get back to Thompson afterwards."

"Okay. I'm going to give you a brief rundown on what we've learnt here." She recapped the terrible incident Elizabeth had just had the courage to convey to her and the other information she'd imparted about the brothers. "Now, you can see why I need more hands on deck. There's too much information for us to sift through, just the three of us. If possible, I'd like to wrap this up tonight. Strike swiftly."

"I get that. Let's hope we can nail these bastards, and soon."

"Okay, I'll be in touch again soon. We'll nip over to see Helen Davis after we've finished here. You do what's necessary to action the team at your end. As soon as Jill gets there, providing she doesn't turn the plea down of course, get her to call me and I'll get Carla to relay the information we've gathered about the brothers."

"Will do, boss. Good luck."

"You too."

Sara inhaled a deep breath and then headed back into the lounge. Three sets of expectant eyes turned her way. "No news, not in the respect that we've arrested him anyway. Quite the opposite, we've learned that another young woman has possibly gone missing."

Elizabeth gasped and shook her head. "That's terrible. Please, you must try your best to find her."

"We will, I promise. Do we have all the information now?"

Carla nodded. "I think we're done, aren't we, Elizabeth?"

"I believe so. I hope it helps you to arrest the... I'm sure you can add an appropriate name at the end."

"We can. I can't thank you enough for having the courage to come forward today, Elizabeth."

"I couldn't sit here and do nothing, not when there are lives at risk."

"It was admirable of you to get in touch, nonetheless. We're going to get off now, looks like a busy evening ahead of us." Carla joined her at the doorway. "Stay there, we'll see ourselves out."

They left the house and jumped back in the car. Sara entered the postcode for Helen Davis' address into the satnav and went over the details of the conversation she'd had with Craig.

"Bugger, we're about to devastate this woman's life."

"I know. I can't say I'm looking forward to holding this conversation. I've also told Craig to call the rest of the team in."

"Really? You're adamant we're closing in on the brothers?"

"Aren't you?"

"I think there's a lot of research to be done before we can even consider that."

"Hence my calling the team in. We can't be out here breaking bad news to a victim's family and do the necessary research at the same time."

"I know. It's an unprecedented situation, I grant you."

The next hour or so was one of the most harrowing of Sara's career. She had the misfortune of telling Helen Davis that her daughter had lost her life. Sara instantly corroborated it was Layla whose body had been found when she saw all the photos of the young woman dotted around the lounge. When Helen broke down and her husband, Andy, asked how their daughter had died, Sara's heart went out to the couple when she revealed the truth.

"What? You suspect she was thrown or fell from a plane?" her father asked, dumbfounded.

"We believe so, yes."

"You're telling us it appears she was abducted like these other girls who have tragically gone missing this week?" Andy probed.

"Apparently, yes."

"How many of those have ended up... dead?"

"It's hard to say. To date, only your daughter's body has been discovered."

"Oh God. This is all too much for me to take. I need my daughter, I need to see her, to make sure it's her," Helen mumbled, clearly overwhelmed.

"I was about to suggest the same. I can contact the mortuary, get the all-clear from them for you to view your daughter's body."

Helen broke down in tears again and nodded.

Andy hugged his wife and ran a soothing hand over her hair. "Hush now. We'll get to see her again soon, love."

"But it'll be for the last time," Helen's words came out staggered as if she was having problems breathing.

Sara knew she needed to get back to the station, but she also realised she had a responsibility towards the couple. After breaking such news, she couldn't just run within seconds. She had more compassion within her to see things through.

She and Carla listened to the couple's grief-filled anecdotes of what their daughter had got up to as a child for the next thirty minutes until Sara's phone rang. She excused herself and went into the hallway to take the call.

"Hi, boss, it's Jill. Just to let you know we're all here. Craig told me to ring you the second I got in."

"Thanks, Jill. This could be it. I need you to do some research for me on Burrows Finances. We believe the suspects own the firm, Harvey and Daniel Burrows. Let me know what you find out about them. The most important thing we need to do is find out Harvey's car details. Once you have that, I need either Craig or Will to try and locate the car on the ANPR system."

"I'll get on it right away, boss and call you back with any news."

Sara lowered her voice. "We're almost done here. We'll be heading back to base soon."

"Hopefully, we'll have the information you're after by the time you arrive."

"Let's hope so. I'll see you soon."

Sara ended the call and made her excuses to leave. "Sorry, I'm urgently needed back at the station." Carla left her seat and joined her at the door.

Andy squeezed his wife and walked towards them. "Is it good news? Have you found the suspect you're after?"

"Possibly. I need to get back to make sure. Again, I'm sorry for your loss. I'll make the arrangements with the mortuary and ask them to contact you soon."

Andy opened the front door and shook their hands. "Thank you for what you're doing for us. Please, catch the culprit before he can damage anyone else's life."

"We're going to do our very best, I promise."

12

$\mathcal{H}$arvey arrived at the cottage. Furious that everything had been left up to him now. He exited the car and opened the boot. Nicola was lying there, her eyes wide with fear, staring up at him. Her pleas were muffled through the gag.

"Don't wriggle. If you do, it'll make things worse, and I'll probably drop you. No skin off my nose, sweetheart, you'll be the one who will end up with the broken bones."

The woman took his threat seriously and remained still and rigid. He heaved her out of the car, and a twinge appeared in his lower back due to his exertions. He placed her on the ground and stretched out the kink. Realising that her feet were bound, he roughly grabbed her arm and threw her over his shoulder. "Someone needs to lose weight." Even though she was a possible size eight or ten, he couldn't resist the dig, aware of what effect his words could have on the woman.

He entered the house and pressed the key fob to lock the car. Once inside, he placed the woman in one of the kitchen chairs. She stared at him, resembling a startled deer caught in a hunter's sightline. "I'll take you through to meet the others soon. First, I need to make them some food; it's been a while since they've had anything to eat. This place isn't a prison where you get three square meals a day. Around here, you get fed and watered when I remember, so don't expect to get fat while you're here."

There was no response from his latest asset. He boiled the kettle and got the cups ready. Then he went to the freezer and withdrew three meals. He didn't care what they were. He defrosted them in the microwave and then heated them up for three minutes, not caring if they were cooked thoroughly or not. "You girls need to appreciate what you're given." He pulled her to her feet and hauled her onto his shoulder again. It would have been easier to have untied her bindings, but the consequences rattled through his mind. *What if she lashed out? Caught me with a blow and knocked me out? There are knives everywhere, it wouldn't take much for her to kill me. No, it's better this way, not for the old back, though. A good soak in the bath tonight will put things right.* He opened the door to the room where the other girls were. He switched on the light, and they scurried to the back of the bed, huddled together against the cold wall behind them.

"Another friend to keep you company. I'll leave you to introduce yourselves while I fetch your meals." He deposited the girl on the bed, and it creaked beneath the extra weight of a third person. He went back into the kitchen and took three plastic forks out of the cutlery drawer. He was being cautious, didn't trust the women with metal ones. He could trust no one in this game. Even his own brother, after the way he'd treated him in the past few hours. Once the girls had been given their meals, he went back into the kitchen and placed the call he'd been contemplating and worrying about for a while.

"Hi, Shipman. Yep, it's Harvey. Are we still on for tomorrow?"

"Yep. Transport has all been arranged at my end. Have you got the correct number of girls?"

"I have, three as arranged. Where do you want me to make the drop?"

"I'll text you the details. Same phone number?"

"That's right."

"Okay. Hold tight. I'll get back to you later." Shipman hung up.

"Fuck. I need more than that, arsehole. I hate being in limbo, babysitting the fucking girls like this."

Tiredness overwhelmed him. He rested his head on his arms on the table and promptly fell asleep.

~

"Hello, I'm Nicola. I don't mind confessing that I'm petrified. How long have you been here? Why is he holding us here?"

"I'm Amber and this is Davina. We've been here a few days now, one day merges with the next. With no windows, we're struggling to know if it's day or night out there. He keeps the light off in here. You asked why he's holding us here. The truth is, we haven't been told."

"Has he… umm… done anything to you?"

"Do you mean has he raped us?"

Nicola nodded. "Yes. Has he?"

"Yes, a number of times. We'll try and stop it happening to you," Amber replied.

"Oh God, I don't want him near me." Nicola noticed how dead Davina's eyes were and sobbed at the thought of him touching her.

"Hush now, none of that. What will be will be."

Nicola wiped her nose on her sleeve. "But why is he keeping us here, is it just for the sex?"

Amber paused, taking her first mouthful of her meal and replied, "We don't know, he hasn't mentioned anything. There's usually two of them."

With no more words to share, the three of them began eating their meals; it was lukewarm, cold even at the bottom, but Nicola tucked in all the same, not knowing when her next meal would be supplied. He'd already warned her of that.

"Oh shit! Do they both… you know?"

"It's better if you don't think about that, it'll make you go out of your mind."

"How do we get out of here?" Nicola asked, her gaze swiftly scanning the square room.

"We haven't come up with a plan yet. He has us chained to the bed."

Nicola glanced down at her legs. "Mine aren't."

The three girls stared at each other. "This could be good news. One of us could pretend she's ill, we trick him and pounce on him. The odds are in our favour, three to one if the other man isn't around. Once we've killed him, Nicola, you could set us free," Amber suggested.

"We have chains at our disposal," Davina chimed in.

"That's right. We could lure him in and chain him up," Nicola suggested before her heart sank. "What if he has a knife or gun and retaliates? Shit! I can't do this."

Amber stroked the back of Nicola's hand. "What's the alternative? I think I've probably been here nearly a week already. I'm starving. Look at the tripe he feeds us. We haven't had a shower or been allowed to use the loo since we got here. Our personal hygiene sucks. I can't live like this much longer, I just can't. And we have no idea where any of this is going to lead. It's tearing me apart, the not knowing."

"Where do you go to the toilet?" Nicola glanced around the room.

Amber reached under the bed and pulled out a bucket that stank.

Nicola retched. "Fuck, no, don't tell me that. Shit, I wondered what the smell was. How degrading is that?"

"It's true. He expects us to use the bucket, depriving us of our dignity." Amber shoved the disgusting vessel back under the bed.

"I'm scared about what his intentions are. He can't keep us here indefinitely, can he? Have either of you tried to figure out how to get out of here? We have to do something. My father always taught me it was better to fight than accept the inevitable, if someone is taking advantage of you."

"That's all well and good. Maybe it would be worth a try, but on the other hand, what if we screw things up and he punishes us further? As in kills us?" Amber replied.

Silence descended and the girls finished their meals. "That was vile. I have no idea what I've just eaten," Nicola announced.

"Hey, be thankful for what you got, that was one of the better meals this fucker has given us."

"I don't want to be here. We have to escape, we just have to."

"We'll put our heads together. If he comes in, make sure you tuck your legs under you. If he spots that he's forgotten to tether you, then we've had it," Davina said.

Nicola put their containers on the floor and then tucked her legs underneath her. The girls chatted, telling each other about their families and the jobs they held in order to while away the hours that followed.

13

Sara rang Mark on the way back to the station to make him aware of the situation and told him not to expect her home anytime soon.

"Thanks for letting me know. Sara, stay safe, don't put yourself in harm's way unnecessarily."

"As if I'd do that. Honestly, I've got an excellent team around me, they've all stepped up to the plate when I needed them most. Enjoy the rest of your evening."

"I will. Take care and no heroics, promise me."

"I promise. Carla will ensure that doesn't happen, won't you, partner?"

Carla tittered. "I'll make sure she stays out of trouble, Mark."

"Thanks, Carla."

Sara tutted. "I love you. See you later."

"Me too. I'll be thinking about you."

She ended the call. "Soppy bugger."

"He's adorable. Someone to treasure for sure."

"Yeah, you're right."

She parked in her usual place at the station then she and Carla ran through the reception area and upstairs to the incident room. "We're back. Don't all shout at once, what have you got for us?"

Jill raised her hand. "I've managed to locate the brother's address, Harvey's car registration and where their business is located in the city centre."

"Well done, you. Right, I think we need to set up some surveillance on the brother's address. Will and Marissa, why don't you take that?"

Will and Marissa leapt out of their seats, collected the address from Jill and then tore out of the office.

"Keep in touch," Sara called after them. "Craig, what have you got for me?"

"I put a call out to the patrol vehicles in the area to be on the lookout for Nicola Thompson's car. Five minutes ago, one of the patrols alerted me that her car had been spotted in a lay-by down a country lane. So, once Jill gave me Harvey's registration number, I entered the details in the system and spotted his car a few miles from the area of her abandoned vehicle. Thinking it was too much of a coincidence, I'm in the process of tracking his car at present."

"Great. Where is he?" Sara asked.

"At the moment, I've got him heading out through Ludlow."

"Ludlow? Shit, out of our jurisdiction. I'll get on to our associates in the Shropshire police. I had it in mind to do it, anyway. That's where the plane has been landing. Keep me up to date, Craig."

"Sure will, boss."

There was an air of excitement and positivity running through the team. Sara asked Carla to get them a round of coffees and left a handful of coins on the nearest desk on her way into her office to place the call.

Once she'd been put through to a DI Lloyd who was manning the office, she relayed the details she had regarding the plane and what Craig had informed her about Harvey's car and which direction it was heading in.

"Okay, let me take a look at the ANPR system from our direction and I'll get back to you as soon as I find anything."

"Are you sure it's not putting you out, DI Lloyd?"

"Not at all, and it's Ray. I've been twiddling my thumbs all evening, so you're doing me a favour."

"We can't have that, can we? I appreciate your willingness to help us."

"Can't have dirtbags like him on the loose, not in our county."

"Nor in ours. Thanks for agreeing to work with me. Keep in touch."

"Ditto, if you manage to spot him before I do."

"I'll get Craig to call you straight away. I'm sensing we're close to finding this bastard, it would be a shame to let him slip out of our grasp now."

"It won't be through anything I've done, I assure you. Teamwork is the dreamwork."

"Let's hope you're right about that." She left the office again and gave Craig DI Lloyd's direct number. "Call him with any updates, he'll be checking from his end." She paused and sipped at the coffee Carla handed her. "I'm inclined to get on the road, just in case."

Her partner frowned. "Will it be worth it?"

"Why not? We're aware of which direction he's heading in."

"I don't know, I have my doubts. What if, hear me out here… what if he's realised we're onto him and is leading us astray, or worse than that, into a trap?"

Sara sighed. "I know you're right, but my head is telling me one thing and my heart another. All I keep thinking about is the girls. He's keeping them somewhere, who's to say where and what conditions they're having to endure?"

Carla sipped at her coffee and rolled her eyes. "Logical answer, I suppose. Why isn't our job ever simple?"

"How many serving police officers ask that question throughout their career?"

"Want to know what I would do?"

"Carla, we work as a team. Bat ideas around, you know you can always speak freely. Go on."

"Of course it depends on what happens with Will and Marissa, but I would bring the brother in, if he's at home."

"And if he's not?"

"Then we'd be forced to rethink things."

Sara contemplated her partner's suggestion for a few seconds, tapping her finger against her cheek as she thought. "That totally makes sense. Bring him in for questioning in the hope he gives up the location. On the flip side, if Harvey finds out we have his brother locked up in a cell, it could send him over the edge. Bearing in mind what he did to Elizabeth and that he probably killed Layla. We know he's got an evil streak."

"Hmm... you're right. I wonder what his intention is with the girls."

"I haven't got the foggiest. Elizabeth didn't hint that he was warped at all, evil yes, but not a sexual deviant, did she?"

"Nope. So near and yet so damn far, still. This case is doing my head in."

*T*hirty minutes later, the surveillance team touched base with them. "Go ahead, Will, I have you on speaker."

"We're outside Daniel Burrows' house now, boss. There's a car in the drive and we keep seeing movement inside."

"What sort of house is it? By that I mean, could there possibly be a basement to the property?"

"Not from what I can tell. Want me to get out and take a closer look?"

"No, hang fire on that. Craig has managed to spot his brother's car on the system, he's in Shropshire. I've got our colleagues up there keeping a close eye on him from their end."

"Sounds promising. If they've been working as a pair throughout, it begs the question why they feel the need to split up now."

"Yeah, that's the part that concerns me."

"What about bringing him in for questioning?" Will suggested hesitantly.

"Yeah, Carla said the same. Okay, bring him in. Don't do it until backup arrives, I'll organise that for you now."

"Rightio. We'll let you know when we're back at the station."

Sara ended the call and rang down to the reception area. She instructed the desk sergeant to send a patrol car to Daniel's address and she explained the reason behind her request. He assured her he would deal with it and send officers who were Taser-trained just in case any aggro kicked off.

She paced the room until she received a text from Will to say they were bringing Daniel in without any resistance.

"He's on his way," she conveyed to the rest of the team. "I'm not sure what to expect now, Will said he didn't put up a fight. Does that sound like an evil kidnapper-cum-murderer to you?"

Carla and the rest of the team all shook their heads.

"I'm nipping to the loo before he gets here. I know, too much information. Hey, guys, sharing is caring, remember that."

Everyone laughed.

*W*hen she came out of the toilet, Carla was waiting for her in the hallway. "Thought I'd give you some privacy in there. Daniel's here. They've taken him to the interview room."

"Let's go see what the shit has to say, then."

Sara was shocked when she opened the door to find Daniel with his head bowed. He was sitting at the table with a duty solicitor by his side. He wasn't what she expected at all. His clean-shaven appearance and demeanour caught her off-guard for a second. Will and Marissa vacated the chairs opposite him to make way for Sara and Carla. Their colleagues left the room. In the corner stood a burly six-foot male, uniformed officer.

Carla started the interview disc by announcing who they were.

"Hi, Daniel, thanks for agreeing to come in and help us with our enquiries." Sara started off playing the nice cop.

Daniel shrugged. "No idea why I'm here."

"Really? And yet, my colleagues said you didn't resist the invitation to join us."

"I figured there wouldn't be much point. What do you want from me?"

Sara opened the manila folder she'd fetched with her. She slid the picture of his brother and Layla Davis in front of him. "Two people in this picture, who are they?"

He stared at the photo, long and hard, and then his gaze drifted up to meet hers. "My twin and I think her name is Layla."

"You mean, *was* Layla. You're aware that she's dead, aren't you?"

He fidgeted in his chair and ran a hand through his short brown hair. "Yeah, I am. I had nothing to do with that, so don't even try pinning it on me."

"Explain that statement, if you will?"

He paused, chewed his lip a few times and shook his head. "I can't."

"Can't or *won't*? Were you there?"

"Sort of."

"Come on, Daniel, you're going to have to give me more than that."

He hesitated, fiddled with his hands for a moment and then admitted, "I was there, but I didn't realise what was going on. I'm not going to take the—"

"Fall? Is that what you were about to say? Just like Layla fell from the plane you and your brother own?"

His eyes widened in shock. "You know?"

"Of course we do. Why? Why throw her from the plane?"

"I didn't. I was too busy flying the damn thing at the time."

"How can you continue to fly with the door open?"

"With difficulty, that's how. He went too far this time. We've barely spoken since."

"You're referring to Harvey?"

"Yes."

"Why aren't you talking?"

"I've just told you why, because of that incident."

"You didn't want to kill her?"

He shook his head. "It wasn't in the plan, no."

"What *plan* would that be?" Daniel fell silent, as if he realised he'd said too much already. Sara decided to ask a different question with the intention of returning to that particular one later. "Where were you travelling to, and for what reason?"

"Shropshire."

"The reason behind your flight?"

"I can't tell you that."

"Back to the 'I won't tell you' statement. Why, Daniel? Why are you persisting in not telling us the facts? We're onto what you and your brother have been up to, it's only a matter of time before we find Harvey and the girls. We're aware that you landed at an airfield close to Church Stretton."

His bowed head shot up. Sara fixed gazes with him. "You know? How?"

Sara laughed. "Apart from being a shit-hot detective, I have ways of seeking the truth. We're closing in on your brother. We have teams in Hereford, heading to Shropshire now to join our colleagues there. We've also dispatched an Armed Response Team. You could save us a lot of trouble and help your brother out by giving us the location where the girls are being kept."

He turned his head to the side a little and stared at the corner of the room. "I can't... he'd kill me if he found out."

"And who's likely to tell him? I won't, I swear to you. Save us all a lot of hassle, Daniel, tell us where he's hiding the girls." Daniel scratched his head, as if he was mulling over what to do for the best. Sara sensed he was on the verge of cracking. "The girls, none of them deserved this, or did they, Daniel?"

"No. I said the same, but Harvey insisted we were doing the right thing."

"In what respect? What's happened to the girls?"

He squeezed his forehead with his shaking hand. "He's gone too far. I never wanted to be involved. He persuaded me it was in our best interest."

"Best interest? Are we talking financially here?"

He nodded and Sara's gut clenched. "He's going to sell them?"

Daniel remained silent, his gaze flicking between Sara, Carla and the duty solicitor.

"Daniel?" Sara urged.

"Yes. I said I didn't want any part of it. He warned me what would happen if I backed out."

"Which was what?"

"Our parents know nothing about this. He threatened to tell them. If they found out what we were up to, they would cut us off completely."

"But they're wealthy, aren't they? Why does Harvey need the money if your family is rich?"

"It's not like that. Mother and Father insisted that we should make our own way in this world. Harvey rejected that idea. He wants money, lots of it, without having to earn it."

"But you run a business together. You're financial experts, aren't you?"

"Yes. Have you seen the state of the markets lately? The pandemic caused people to be more cautious with their money. Not only that, many of them lost their jobs. That's had a devastating effect on our business."

Sara fell back in her seat. "You're kidding me? You're struggling for money, so you decided to kidnap some girls to sell them to the highest bidder?"

His hand shook and he wiped it across his face. "Yes, I suppose you could put it like that. I didn't want to get involved."

"But you flew the plane, in my opinion, you're a hundred percent involved in this scheme."

"I'm not. We've fallen out. I've told him I want nothing more to do with him."

"If that's the case, tell us where he is, Daniel. If you have any conscience at all, which by the sounds of it, you have. For God's sake, give us the location. Or is it too late?"

"No. The handover isn't going to take place for a few days. Saying that, Harvey could possibly alter the arrangements."

"Tell us where the property is. Please consider the women, they didn't ask to be involved in this. You think it's right to rob someone so young of their freedom? Do you have any idea what these girls will be subjected to if they're sold?"

He gasped and shook his head. "I never really thought about the consequences until yesterday. Please, I'm not to blame for this, he is."

"Help us! Before it's too late."

He covered his face with his hands and sobbed.

Sara snatched a quick glance at Carla who nodded, urging her not to give up.

Banging her fist on the table, Sara shouted, "If you have an ounce of decency left in your body, you'll tell us where those girls are before Harvey gets the chance to move them. He's on his way there by car now, with yet another girl. For Christ's sake, do the right thing, Daniel. Save those girls from a life of torture and grief."

He slumped back in his chair and whispered, "Give me a pen and paper."

Carla pushed her notebook in front of him and he scribbled down the address. Sara snatched it, raced out of the room and took the stairs two at a time. "I've got it. Craig, get DI Lloyd on the phone for me."

Craig sprang into action, and within seconds, he handed the phone to her. "Hi, it's DI Ramsey in Hereford. I've got a possible address."

"Only possible? How accurate do you think it is?"

"His brother gave it to me. He's emotionally wrought and full of guilt, I get the impression he's trying to do the right thing. Apparently, he's fallen out with his brother. The girls are being held until a rendezvous can take place, it's due soon. We have to get to them quickly. I'm going to get on the road now. I'll meet you at the location. Do you have the clout to arrange an ART?"

"Of course. Okay, I'll sort things out at this end and meet you at the location on one proviso."

"What's that?"

"We make the arrest."

"No way. My team and I have done all the legwork on this, no way!"

He laughed. "Okay, I was pulling your leg. The bastard is all yours. I'll action everything as soon as I hang up. What's the address?"

Sara gave him the details, he confirmed he knew the location, which was pretty remote, and hung up.

She then patted Craig on the shoulder. "Come with me. We'll leave Carla to deal with Daniel."

"Cool. I mean, that's great, boss. Want me to drive?"

"Insinuating you'll get us there quicker?"

"I happen to enjoy driving in the dark, not many women I know feel the same way."

She rolled her eyes. "That'll teach you to assume. I'm fine in the dark. However, I am going to take you up on your offer. We'll go in my car. Jill, can you let Carla know?"

"I'll do it now. Good luck with your mission. I hope you catch the fucker."

They tore down the stairs and out to the car. She pressed the key fob, then threw the keys to Craig. He adjusted the seat after catching his knee on the steering wheel. "If you don't mind me saying, boss, you're a short arse."

"Bloody cheek. Good things come in small packages, didn't your mother ever tell you that?"

He laughed. "I'll take your word for it and hope my knee heals swiftly."

"Stop whingeing. Go, Craig. We need to get there, fast. I hate to miss out on any action when an arrest is made."

"I hope we're not too late. He's got a couple of hours' head start on us."

"All the more reason to use the siren."

He grinned and flicked the switch once they joined the main road.

Sara watched the satnav clock count down. "Another ten minutes."

"I hope the others haven't got the jump on us."

"I told Lloyd to hold back until we got there."

Nine.

Eight.

Seven.

Six.

Five.

Four.

Three.

Two.

One. "The road must be around here somewhere," Craig grumbled.

Peering into the darkness, Sara caught sight of something. "Wait, what's that? Is it an interior light I can see?"

They drove closer and it soon became apparent that there were three vehicles waiting at the side of the road.

Craig drew up in front of the first one, and Sara leapt out of the car. Craig switched off the engine and followed her.

"Ray Lloyd?"

"DI Ramsey?"

She recognised his voice, smiled and shook his hand. "Have you been here long?"

"Around thirty minutes, not too long. You made good time."

"Thanks to my speedy colleague. What about the ART? Did you manage to get one assigned?"

"They should be here soon. They're around five minutes away, last time I spoke to the commanding officer."

"Good. I take it the house is up this lane?"

"That's right. I sent one of my lads up there to have a recce. His car is up there, we matched up the details to what you gave me to be sure."

"Excellent news. I hope he hasn't got wind of us being here. I fear what might happen to the girls if he gets stressed."

"That's why we need to leave it to the ART. Do you know if he's armed?"

"Damn, no. I forgot to ask his brother. I think we should presume he is."

"Good thinking. Did his brother say what their motive is behind the abductions?"

"Yeah, primarily to sell the girls for money as their business has suffered during the pandemic."

"What the fuck? I've heard it all now. Sick bastards."

"Yep. Is this them?" Sara pointed at an approaching vehicle.

"Looks like it to me."

Sara and Ray marched over to the vehicle. The commanding officer held a hand up, preventing them from getting any closer until he'd relayed certain orders to his team. Then he addressed them. "Who's in charge here?"

"It's my patch, DI Ray Lloyd, but DI Ramsey needs to make the arrest as the suspect is from Hereford."

"Okay. Well, I'm taking over control for now. Where do we stand on the suspect? Is he armed?"

"We're not sure," Sara replied. "Ray's colleague has confirmed the suspect is at the residence. We need to be cautious, there are at least three girls inside the house, that we're aware of."

"We'll go in as rapidly and as efficiently as we can. We're not in the habit of putting innocent people at risk. How many are we looking at? One male or possibly more?"

"That's correct, one male. I have a picture of him if that will help?"

"It will."

Sara dug out her phone and enlarged the photo she'd snapped of Harvey with Layla. "He killed this woman, she's the only one, we believe at this point."

"Okay, then my guys need to be aware that we're dealing with a highly dangerous individual."

"I suppose so. Yes. Please, if you can take him alive, it'll make my life easier."

"We're not like our American counterparts, we always do our best to take suspects alive. Leave it to us." He walked away and gathered his troops for a final meeting before they set off up the lane.

"I wish I could be there," Sara muttered.

"Yeah, me too," Ray admitted. "If there's a sense of imminent danger from this guy, then maybe it's just as well that we remain here."

Sara inhaled a large breath, her gaze fixed on the entrance to the dark country lane.

A few minutes later, shouting filled the cold night air. A shot was fired, then nothing. Sara couldn't hold back any longer. She bolted up the lane, despite Ray and Craig trying their best to hold her back.

She detested Harvey on sight. To look at him, he seemed a trustworthy businessman, but knowing that he was a serial kidnapper and had killed a woman caused Sara to shudder slightly. She brushed her emotions aside and said, "Thank God. Where are the girls?" she asked the commanding officer.

"We're searching the rest of the property now. He was asleep in the kitchen. We managed to jump him before he had a chance to move."

"What about the shot that was fired?"

"A warning shot, he tried to run."

Sara glared at Harvey and grinned. "Silly boy!"

"Screw you!" Came back his vicious retort. The armed officers took him back to the cars.

Sara rushed into the cottage in search of the girls. "Hello, anyone here?"

Another armed officer appeared in the doorway. "We've found them. They appear to be shaken up, but okay nevertheless."

"Can I see them?"

He stepped aside and gestured for her to join him. "Down here on the right. How they survived the bloody cold is beyond me."

Sara shivered as the intensive chill seeped into her bones. "Shit! It's freezing."

"It's worse in the room they were kept in. There's a bare wall at the back, the house is dug into the hillside."

Sara frowned, finding it hard to imagine how a room described like that would be until she walked in and saw it for herself. "Bloody hell. We need to get some blankets round these girls, pronto!"

"I'll see what we've got in the van. Want me to ring for an ambulance?"

"Yes. Top priority. Now they're safe, they need to be checked over." The officer left. Sara took a few paces closer to the bed. "Are you all okay? Any injuries we should be concerned about?"

"No, we're okay in that respect. We're so glad you found us. What will happen now?"

Sara smiled at the girl she knew as Amber. "We'll get you assessed at the hospital and then reunite you with your families."

The girls' resilient façades crumbled before her eyes. They gripped each other's hands, hugged and sobbed.

A large lump lodged itself in Sara's throat, and she had to turn away from them to hide the tears of relief trickling down her cheeks. After a few moments, she ran her cuff over her eyes, fixed a smile in place and motioned for the girls to join her. Two of them pointed out they were chained at the ankle. "Damn, okay. Let me get that sorted now. I'll be right back."

She met the armed officer she had spoken to before in the damp hallway. He had a pile of metallic blankets in his arms. "Two of the girls are chained to the bed, can you help with that?"

"Yep. You take these. I'll go back to the van and see what I can find to resolve the problem."

"Or you could get the key off Burrows." Sara grinned.

"Now there's a thought. I'll be right back either way."

She wrapped the blankets around each of the girls' shoulders. Their gratitude was clear to see. "We'll have you out of here soon."

The officer reappeared with the key to unlock the chains and released two of the girls from their ghastly restraints. Once they heard the sirens approaching, Sara and the officer escorted the girls out of the cottage and into the ambulance.

Craig was close by. Sara stepped back and joined him. "We need to contact the station, let them know."

Craig smiled. "I've done it already. Carla's awaiting a call from you before she rings the families."

"Excellent. I'll get in touch in a second. I just need to have a word with the paramedics first." One of the paramedics spotted them and came towards them.

"They appear to be okay, we'll take them in and get them checked over, just in case."

"We need to get them back to their families in Hereford."

"We'll be taking them to the local hospital in Church Stretton. I don't think we can offer any assistance in sending them home, sorry."

"That's not your concern, I can arrange transportation. Thanks for your help."

"All in a day's work." He returned to the ambulance.

Sara surveyed the frantic activity ahead of her during her call to Carla. "Hi, it's me. We've got them all. They're on their way to be checked out at the hospital."

"Thank God. Do you want me to call the families now?"

"Yes. We also need to arrange some form of transport to get the girls back to Hereford, can you do that as well?"

"I'm on it. What about Harvey Burrows?"

"He's been arrested. We'll be bringing him back ourselves. We'll be setting off soon."

"Drive carefully. Congratulations on another case well solved, Sara."

"Teamwork, Carla. All down to the fantastic team I have around me." *And I've got to let someone go after all this dies down!*

She pushed the thought aside and smiled at Craig. "Let's get back to base."

EPILOGUE

The journey back to Hereford was a quiet one. Being in the confined space with the perpetrator made Sara's skin crawl. Although she attempted to ask Harvey several questions en route, he just stared at her and refused to answer. Finally, she said, "I don't think the bank of mummy and daddy will be able to get you out of this shit, Mr Burrows."

He harrumphed a retort, mumbled something under his breath and leaned his head back against his seat.

Once they arrived at the station, Sara and Craig escorted Harvey down the corridor to Interview Room One. They were joined by his own solicitor soon after. It proved to be a waste of time as Harvey continually spouted only two words throughout the interview, 'no comment'.

In the end, Sara gave up and threw him in a cell. She willed her tired legs to carry her up the stairs to the incident room. "We did it, team. Come on, I say we call it a night. He can stew in a cell, and I'll try to question him again on Monday."

Carla grinned. "I don't blame you. I agree, let's go home."

.   .   .

he following day Sara was served breakfast in bed by her ever-thoughtful husband. He fussed over her most of the day, insisting that she should chill out in front of the TV all day after such a hectic week. He spoiled her rotten, cooked her a full roast dinner, insisting she should stay out of the kitchen until he'd finished. It was one of the best cuts of beef she'd ever eaten.

They spent the next few hours cuddled up on the sofa, munching on a box of salted caramel Lindor chocolates that had mysteriously jumped into Sara's shopping trolley the week before.

At around three, their chill-out time together had to be sacrificed when Mark received an emergency call to attend a puppy who had been run over.

Rather than twiddle her thumbs until Mark returned home, and with her body and mind still pumping with excess adrenaline, Sara decided to go for a drive. Something niggling her mind led her to Gary's home. She pulled up and wondered if she had done the right thing, coming here.

He arrived home shortly after. She spotted him swaggering up the road, carrying his gym bag. She reached for the handle to get out, but paused when she saw a man jump out in front of him. Sara ducked down in her seat and observed the angry exchange between them for several minutes. The stranger jabbed Gary in the stomach, and he doubled over. The man stood firm and continued to shout at him. Finally, with Gary still bent over, the man stormed off.

With an ever-enquiring mind, Sara leapt out of the car and crossed the road to speak to Gary. His eyes widened when he spotted Sara. He tried to straighten up and winced.

"What was that all about?" she demanded.

"Nothing!"

"Nothing? Don't give me that bullshit."

"Just leave it. This has nothing to do with you."

"But everything to do with Carla, I'm guessing."

A sheepish expression descended. He brushed past her towards his house.

Seething, she shouted, "If I find out you either attacked her or paid for someone to attack her, I promise you, I won't rest until you're behind bars."

He trotted up to his front door, looked over his shoulder and sneered, "You know nothing!" He slammed the front door behind him. Leaving Sara wondering what he'd meant.

She'd find out soon enough – she was determined to get to the bottom of this particular mystery.

THE END

*P*erhaps you'd also consider reading another of my most popular series? Grab the first book in the Justice series here, CRUEL JUSTICE

DI Sara Ramsey will return with a brand new case, early in 2021.

KEEP IN TOUCH WITH M A COMLEY

Pick up a FREE novella by signing up to my newsletter today.
https://BookHip.com/WBRTGW

BookBub
www.bookbub.com/authors/m-a-comley

Blog
http://melcomley.blogspot.com

Join my special Facebook group to take part in monthly giveaways.

Readers' Group

Made in the USA
Las Vegas, NV
27 February 2021

18723486R00115